P9-CAO-552

A KILLER NECKLACE

Fashionation with Mystery #2

Melodie Campbell & Cynthia St-Pierre

A KILLER NECKLACE
Fashionation with Mystery #2

Copyright © 2015 by Melodie Campbell and Cynthia St-Pierre. All Rights Reserved.

IF YOU RECEIVED THIS BOOK FREE VIA A WEBSITE DOWNLOAD ON A SHARE OR TORRENT SITE, YOU HAVE AN ILLEGAL COPY AND CAN BE PROSECUTED FOR COPYRIGHT THEFT.

Copyright is a matter we take seriously. Our authors and our publishing team work hard to produce quality books for people who will appreciate them. We often have discounts and sales so that ANYONE CAN AFFORD OUR EBOOKS.

No part of this publication may be reproduced, stored in a retrieval system, or transmitted, in any form or by any means, electronic, mechanical, photocopying, recording, or otherwise, without prior written permission from the author.

This is a work of fiction. Names, characters, places and incidents either are the product of the author's imagination or are used fictitiously. And any resemblance to actual persons, living, dead (or in any other form), business establishments, events, or locales is entirely coincidental.

www.fashionationwithmystery.com

FIRST EDITION Trade Paperback

Imajin Books

October 15, 2015

ISBN: 978-1-77223-141-0

Cover designed by Ryan Doan, www.ryandoan.com

Praise for A Killer Necklace

"5 Stars for *A Killer Necklace*. After having so enjoyed Gina, Becki and Tony in *A Purse to Die For*, *A Killer Necklace* does not disappoint. The story races along, unfolding around truly believable, and lovable, characters. The final chapters are hard to put down as the pace picks up, moving steadily and convincingly towards the climax. Now my only question is: 'What's next and when will they be back?'" —Lorna Gray, author of *Finding Daylight*

"Once again Cynthia and Melodie have seamlessly combined their words and talent to create another fun adventure for Gina and her friend Becki. A wonderful cast of characters to keep you enthralled every step of the way." —Nanci M. Pattenden, author of *Body in the Harbour: A Detective Hodgins Victorian Mystery*

Melodie's Dedication

For my brother Mark.

Cynthia's Dedication

To my newfound family of blood brothers and sisters.

~ ✳ ~

Melodie's Acknowledgements:

Many thanks to Joan, Cathy, Alison, and Cheryl, dear friends and fellow writers who are always there to encourage and support. And warm hugs to Cindy, the best writing partner a gal could have.

Cynthia's Acknowledgements:

Thank you Melodie, Janani, Patti, and members of Write Now @ King; part of my loving community of family, friends, neighbours, doctors, nurses, technicians and volunteers who helped me make it to cancer-free.

Part I

Chapter 1

Shivering is an involuntary physical reaction to temperature. Same with the sweat on my forehead. Humidity.

Tony tried to push down all thoughts that were extraneous to the job at hand—finding Gina.

Entering the one large room, dimly lit by two tiny windows set high in the concrete walls, he flipped the switch on the wall to his left. The glare of bare fluorescents created more contrast, is all. Brighter lights. Deeper shadows.

Despite his training, his heart pumped like he was running uphill.

He always overcame fear with preparation, with experience. But this wasn't fear; this was irrational terror, on behalf of someone he loved more than life itself.

Gina.

She had been investigating a murder. The body of a woman found in a basement, like this one. Now Gina had been forcibly taken.

He tried to convince himself that he had the strength, the training to deal with whatever he found.

Then he stepped forward.

Chapter 2

Three Weeks Earlier...

"Why do you need two suitcases when you're only going away for a weekend?"

Gina could hear the smile in Tony's voice. Still, it made her a titch miffed.

"One is for my wedding dress. I promised to show Becki and the other girls at the shower."

"How come they get to see it and I don't?" He lay on the bed, with both hands behind his head. He still hadn't gotten dressed yet, and the sight of his curly brown hair and bare chest always did something to her.

That's why she couldn't look at him. It was too tempting, and she was on a deadline.

She turned toward the closet, exasperated. "You're the groom, Tony! It's bad luck. You don't get to see my dress until the day of."

He was grinning now. "All the more reason I should just pick you up and run off with you right now. Escape all this nonsense."

Back with another dress, she lay it carefully down on the tissue paper to fold it. It was important she take special care of this new Versace dress. There would be lots of pictures, and Becki even said the local press might be there.

Besides, it wasn't every day you went to your own bridal shower.

"I'm not eloping with you. Becki would kill me."

He snorted. "More likely, she would kill *me.*"

That was true, actually. Gina's adopted aunt would whip him silly with words if he wrecked this wedding they had been planning for months.

Gina turned back to packing her main suitcase.

Becki wasn't really adopted, of course. Becki had been her grandmother's goddaughter. She was more like a cherished older sister to Gina, and although they were not actually related, they looked like they could have been.

Gina's chestnut hair was longer and wavier than Becki's and her body a bit more curvy, but they both had pretty brown eyes. In fact, Gina looked more like Becki than she did her real aunts. And that suited her just fine.

"So you're going all the way up to Black Currant? Why not Langdon Hills? It's half the distance."

She shivered, remembering the last time they had been to Langdon Hills. "Becki is hosting the shower, Tony. Of course it's got to be at her place. If we had it at Grandma's old house, then Carla would be the hostess."

She didn't want that. While she and Aunt Carla had made an uneasy truce, that house wasn't a place of joy anymore. Ian had died there.

She missed her cousin Ian badly.

"I love Black Currant in the spring. It's beautiful up north, when all the greenery starts filling in."

"You're beautiful up north," Tony murmured. "Down south too." He moved like a panther, grabbed both her arms and pulled her down to the bed.

"Tony! I just got dressed."

"So?" he said. "It's fun unwrapping presents."

Tony was ready to leave before she was quite finished packing.

"Can I take those two suitcases down to the car for you?"

She nodded. "Thanks. Have you still got a key?"

He held the sparkly keychain up with one hand. "I'll put them in the trunk for you. But first…"

He came back for one quick final hug.

"You behave," he said, reaching his arms around her and kissing her hair. "Stay away from bears and wilderness men, okay?"

Gina giggled into his chest. "You're all the bear I need."

He swatted her butt, and released her.

"Call me when you get there." He bent to pick up the suitcases.

She watched him leave and couldn't stop herself from smiling.

Tony had thought two suitcases was a lot for a long weekend away. Little did he know that the second suitcase didn't contain her wedding dress.

Pack an haute couture wedding dress in a suitcase? Fold it up like a pair of pants or sweater? Nobody would do that. Well, maybe a man would. She chuckled to herself.

The first suitcase contained her clothes. She had three fancy events to attend, and you just never knew what the weather was going to do up north. The second suitcase contained shoes, two purses, toiletries, books and presents for Becki.

The wedding dress would stay in its long garment bag. She would lay it across the back seat of her car where it wouldn't be crushed.

Just thinking about that dress made her heart race with excitement.

Gina disappeared into the walk-in closet to collect it.

Two hours later, she had cleared the city outskirts and was well on her way to cottage country.

It was a beautiful day for a road trip. Not a cloud in the clear blue sky and the air was that perfect temperature for wearing a summer dress. Often June days in the city were a smoggy sauna. Just a few hours north, it was heaven.

This was Thursday, so before the weekend rush.

She loved visiting Becki and her husband Karl in Black Currant. Ever since Becki married Karl eleven years ago and moved up north, these visits had been the highlight of her summer holidays.

Now *that* had been a wedding to remember. Gina smiled, thinking what a contrast it would seem compared to the posh event that had been planned for her and Tony.

Becki and Karl were married in a small outdoor service at Grandma's Georgian Revival house in Langdon Hills. Becki had worn a simple off-white sheath dress, and had carried fresh flowers, of course. Roses and daisies, as she recalled. Gina remembered grumbling about the bridesmaid dress she had to wear, which was a soft coral shade, and much too plain for her young taste.

But the wedding had been great fun. Grandma had always enjoyed playing the grand matriarch, like in some PBS drama. Aunt Linda was her typical entertaining self, criticising all the gifts that had been displayed on the dining room table. Uncle Reggie had gotten royally plastered as usual.

All the cousins had been there. Gina had danced with both Tony and Ian for most of that night.

Poor Ian. She missed her older cousin so much. Such a horrible thing, to be murdered in cold blood.

And Grandma. Life just wasn't the same without her. Perhaps it had been a natural death after all, like Carla insisted. Even more likely, they would probably never know for sure.

She sighed. The turn off the main highway was up ahead. Just seeing Becki would make her feel better.

Something lumpy lay in the middle of the road, spotted with black. She swerved to avoid it, crossing over into the other lane, and as she did, the crows flew off it.

Some poor animal was now a lifeless carcass. Gina shivered.

Chapter 3

Becki Green peered out her apartment window and gazed down on Main Street. Gina would probably pull her new Camaro into a parking slot right in front of Becki and half-sister Anne's design shop below.

Expect heads to turn, Becki thought. *Shiny red sports cars are not the norm in this town.*

Those same heads would spin like tops once Gina stepped out of her car.

Gina wasn't quite tall enough and maybe a bit too curvy to have worked the runways of the major designers but that didn't stop her from wearing their clothes with a great deal of panache.

Becki turned from her window and headed to the kitchen to set the round table in the dining nook for afternoon tea. It would be just the two of them. Gina would need time to unwind from the long drive. Plus it would be fun to catch up on each other's lives before Karl got home.

Becki carefully laid out a couple April Cornell cotton floral napkins, two vintage teacups and saucers, a gleaming silver teapot and an English three-tiered cake stand that she would soon fill to overflowing with an assortment of homemade scones, delicate tea sandwiches and pastry cream tarts topped with fresh fruit.

She heard a car door slam.

She rushed back to the window and saw a woman directly below with chestnut hair. Had Gina parked in the back? Was that her about to open the door on the street and come tripping up the stairs? From this extreme angle, it was hard to see much more than the top of a head.

No, the woman continued to walk up the Interlock sidewalk until she was out of sight. Imposter Gina.

Becki, enough of this fidgeting! Gina will get here when she gets here. Why are you so anxious? People your age are supposed to remain calm, cool and collected.

She forced herself to sit on her own couch.

Without wanting to, she wondered if she should have chosen a more in-your-face yellow than Buttercream for the living room walls. She adjusted one of the stems in the vase of multi-coloured tulips on the coffee table.

Rap, tap, tap.

Becki jumped to her feet. She flung open her solid wood panel door and there stood her lovely 'niece.'

"Hi Gina!" A huge smile burst onto Becki's face. "How are you? Come in! Come in! How was your trip?" She opened her arms.

"I'm good. So nice to see you!" Gina hugged her back.

When they pulled apart, Becki said, "The kettle has boiled once already. I'll plug it in to reheat and we'll have some tea. You must be starving. Did you eat anything on the way up? So much to talk about with your wedding only three weeks away!"

"Let's go for a walk," Becki suggested after noticing a good hour and a half had slipped by and they were still indoors. "It's beautiful out and I know you love the beach."

"Bring it on!" Gina said jumping up.

"Do you have the right shoes?"

"The path along the lake is crushed gravel, right? My sandals will be fine. If we do decide to walk on the sand, I'll slip them off."

Becki loved showing Gina around Black Currant Bay. The charming small town still boasted nearly all of its original buildings. Gina had been here many times, of course, but the atmosphere changed with every season. The beginning of June was the signal for shopkeepers to display picnic baskets, children's pail sets and straw beach bags brimming with colourful swim suits, whimsical flip-flops and paperback romances.

Only residents knew that the lake wasn't warm enough to actually swim in until July.

They strolled to the bottom of Main Street and right into Harbourfront Park.

Gina cheered, "Dairy Maid is open for business!"

"First day this year."

"Let's come back for a chocolate malted one day before I go."

After strolling up and down the shore, they plumped themselves down at the end of the marina's wood pier, dangled their feet over the edge and looked out over white-capped waves as far as the eye could see.

The sun had started its long descent to the horizon and warmed the right side of their faces. A clean-smelling breeze drifted in off the bay and blew back their hair.

No one appreciates the arrival of summer as much as Canadians, thought Becki.

"I wish life was always so simple," Gina said wistfully.

"Wedding plans got you stressed out?" Becki asked.

"Oh no, I'm looking forward to marrying Tony."

"Well, that's a good thing." Becki didn't press her. She waited for her to divulge more, whenever she was ready.

"It's just that some of the girls at work…"

"Uh-huh?"

"I have a hard time connecting with them."

"You?"

"Yes me." Gina pulled a strand of dark hair from across her eyes. "I mean, they're cordial but it's like they keep this distance between us somehow. I've invited a bunch of them to our wedding, but, I don't know how to put this, it's like they're not really rooting for me. You know what I mean?"

One single advantage comes with age and that's experience. Becki had twenty more years of it than Gina and she knew exactly what it felt like to be on the outside of things sometimes. Oh, she'd made two really good friends since she'd been here in Black Currant Bay but many of the townsfolk couldn't get past their mistrust of 'that hippie vegetarian designer from Toronto.'

"I'm betting they're jealous of how you look." *Might as well state the facts.* "How you dress." Becki was sure Gina knew how much she loved her, so she risked being blunt.

Gina looked at her with a crestfallen expression.

"No question about it, you stand out. I know fashion is your passion. Trouble is, people tend to want others to conform. So they judge and they criticize, hoping to bring everyone to one level of sameness."

"You're not suggesting I—"

"Of course not. Is there anything wrong with beauty or the pursuit of it in all its forms? Art? Music? Fashion?"

"No."

"Are you walking all over people in your effort to express your sense of style?"

"You know me better than that!"

"So shrug off the negativity."

"Sometimes it's hard."

Sometimes it's impossible, Becki thought.

Gina's cellphone rang.

"It's Tony!" she said, looking at the screen. A smile lit up her face. "Excuse me, Becki. Hi babe! Miss me already?"

It was easy to imagine Tony's side of the conversation.

Gina laughed. "Becki's right beside me. We're sitting on the dock with our feet dangling over the edge. Are you jealous?" Then she whispered to Becki, "Tony says hi."

"Hi back," Becki said in sign language.

"In a few minutes we're going to walk over to Becki's client Louisa's house," explained Gina.

Wonderful to see Gina so excited.

"It's right on the water and Becki says that's where the shower is going to take place tomorrow. Not enough room in her apartment and since Louisa offered up her own space... Probably wants to show off her new Beautiful Things kitchen, but Becki says the whole place is fabulous."

Just the slightest hint of a deep male voice floated over to Becki.

"Becki wants to introduce me to Louisa before the big day and of course I want to meet her."

Tony must have said, "Have fun!"

"You too. And I'll be home before you know it."

Pause.

"What?" Gina asked.

Becki noticed a new sharpness to her voice.

"Montreal?"

Chapter 4

"He says Montreal, but who knows what that means?"

Becki smiled indulgently. "Maybe…Montreal?"

The sun was less intense now. Becki breathed in the clean country air and once again thanked the heavens that she and Karl were living out of the city.

She took one last look at the deep blue lake. The walk to Louisa's house would only take them ten minutes at most, but it was time to get going. She gestured for Gina to come with her.

Gina was obviously still steaming about that phone call. Becki sighed. *Best let her get it out of her system, before meeting up with other people.*

"The wedding is only three weeks away. Who knows if he'll get back in time?" Gina grumbled.

"Sweetie, he's only in Montreal."

"Don't bet on it. More likely, he's somewhere in the Middle East. Or Africa. Or Timbuktu."

"Timbuktu *is* in Africa." Becki couldn't resist.

But still, she shared a bit of Gina's angst.

Tony was supposed to have gone 'clean.' No more funny business jetting around the world on behalf of Her Majesty's Colonial Service. *Seems like he couldn't resist one last job.*

This is what she knew Gina was really worried about. Tony had led an exciting life. Would he really be able to give it up and settle back into the role of husband and architect?

Tony had made a promise. This jaunt was probably bending it.

A slight breeze picked up flower blossoms on the sidewalk and whirled them around.

Becki decided to change the subject. "Do you remember meeting Louisa?"

Gina paused. "I think so. At the Christmas tea you held last year. She likes the color blue. I remember she commented on that Missoni I had on."

"Is that why you wore blue today?" Becki asked. It was typical of Gina to remember things like that, and try to please people. Today, she was wearing a gorgeous halter dress in a teal and aqua stained glass pattern.

She brightened. "Yes. It's silly, I know. But I'm sensitive to color myself, so I like to match people with colors they like."

"You mean...?"

"Louisa is blue. Tony is red—he loves it when I wear scarlet. And it suits his personality."

No kidding, Becki thought. "And me?" She had to ask.

"You're...any shade of pink. Like your top. Light and warm and beautiful."

Becki felt her heart lift. Her walk became perkier. "That is a really nice thing to say, Gina."

Gina shrugged. "It's how you are. How I see you, anyway."

Really, Becki thought, *it was the nicest thing anyone had said about her in years.*

And it did the trick. Thoughts of Tony had vanished.

Becki walked briskly, turning the corner.

"You'll like Louisa's house. It's Victorian. One of the big ones on Princess Street. Was a doctor's home originally. Great bones. It has more windows than the usual Victorian mansion, so the light inside is magical. I loved working on it."

Gina grinned. "We're pretty alike, you know. While I go on and on about clothes and color, you think the same about decorating houses."

Becki laughed. "Touché. Well, you'll get to be the judge of this one. It's my masterpiece, you might say."

She turned left. Louisa's house was just ahead.

"Is that it? Wow, it's lovely," said Gina.

And it was. Not quite a mansion, the restored doctor's home featured two tall stories, with perfectly placed gables. The roof had been recently replaced, and the French-blue paint trim beautifully complemented the grey stone on the front of the house. The door was painted soft blue as well.

Becki walked up the flagstone path. It was lined with a plethora of flowers.

"This is only the appetizer. Her real garden is at the back, going down to the lake."

When she reached the door, Becki knocked three times.

They waited.

"I'll try again." She did.

"Maybe Louisa is around the back?"

"Maybe," Becki said. "But's it's unusual. She was expecting us."

This is weird. She peered in through the small diamond shaped window in the door. Nothing. No sign of movement.

Gina stepped nervously from foot to foot.

"I'll just nip around the back and check."

Becki watched her walk to the side of the house. Then she took hold of the doorknob and twisted.

The door swung open.

Now that wasn't too unusual. Many people in Black Currant Bay didn't lock their doors during the day, especially if they were expecting company. It wasn't like the city.

Becki stepped through the doorway. "Louisa?"

No sound came from anywhere in the house.

She moved through the hall and peeked into the large front parlour.

No one.

"Louisa, are you there?"

Nothing. This is definitely strange.

Becki walked to the kitchen at the back. It always lifted her spirits whenever she entered this room. One of her best designs, she noted with satisfaction. Lemon yellow made the most of the southern light that glowed in through the short window over the sink, and the period bay window in the eating area. The tiered curtains with pull backs made a gorgeous frame for the traditional English garden and the lake in the distance.

She could hear the antique clock ticking.

She moved to the sink, looked out and waved to Gina, who was just leaving the back yard.

"I can't find her inside. Any sign?" Becki said through the open window.

Gina shook her head. "I'll check around the other side."

Becki watched her disappear around the corner. She felt the frown lines crease her forehead. Where the heck was Louisa?

She turned, and leaned back against the mocha-streaked granite countertop.

The cellar door stood open. *Perhaps she's doing something downstairs? But you don't do laundry when you have guests coming over.*

It didn't make sense.

Becki hurried to the doorway and looked down.

At the bottom of the painted wooden stairs, lay a body. It was distorted, with twisted limbs, like a rag doll tossed carelessly upon a concrete floor. Red paint seeped from under the camel-clad figure.

"That's not paint," Becki said out loud.

The next few minutes were a blur.

Gina had appeared and taken control. Now, Becki was seated on the parlour sofa. She sat with her head between her legs, fighting to keep hold of her vision.

"I don't know why I got faint like this."

Gina fussed about her, holding a glass of water.

"Keep your head down. I've called 911 and Karl. They'll be here any minute."

Becki moaned. She still didn't feel good. When she tried to lift her head, the room kind of swung around a bit. "Why does it always have to be Karl? He'll get all stern-like and scold me for being here."

"We didn't do anything wrong," Gina said. "She invited us over. And it was probably a good thing we came when we did. Who knows how long she would have been lying there otherwise."

That was true. Luckily, it had only been a few hours since Louisa had called to confirm the time.

Becki shivered. She'd seen the CSI shows.

The trouble with me is I have too much imagination, she thought miserably. *That's what makes me a good designer of course. The ability to imagine things that aren't there yet.*

"Drink this when you're ready." Gina held out the glass.

Becki shook her head. At least, it seemed like she did.

"Do you think she fell?" Gina's voice again.

"What?" Becki tried to lift her head, but Gina's face kept moving in and out of focus.

"Or do you think she was pushed?"

The room stopped moving. Becki snapped out of her reverie. "Why would you ever think that?"

Gina paced the floor.

"She wasn't the only thing at the bottom of the stairs."

Chapter 5

"Um…we might feel better if we wait outside for the cops," Gina suggested.

"No." A new determination had taken hold of Becki. "Even if I can't stay right there with her…with Louisa…I can't leave her alone in the house."

"I understand."

So they sat together quietly in the parlour. When the front door opened and the ambulance crew lumbered in, Gina pointed them in the right direction.

Karl came into the house next with two of his officers. He gave Becki and Gina a brief acknowledgement, motioning that he'd be right back, and then went directly to the scene.

Becki didn't want to know what all the equipment was that the men lugged in and out, or what they were using it for.

Could a half hour have gone by before Karl approached them in the parlour? She noticed his movement across the hardwood floor seemed more of a dejected shuffle than a walk. He was a tall man, with a roughness around the edges that came from living in the northland his whole life.

"What can you tell me?" he asked. He looked from one to the other.

Between the two of them Becki and Gina filled him in about everything from Louisa's original invitation to drop by, to the discovery of her still form.

"Did you check to see if she was alive before you called 911?"

"I did," Gina said.

"No vitals?"

"None."

"Louisa was your client wasn't she, Becki?" Karl asked.

"Yes." Her hand came up and pressed against her lips. "We just recently updated her kitchen."

She had marvelled at the bold urban sensibility of Louisa's vision for this old Victorian in small-town Black Currant Bay.

"What do you know about her?" he asked.

Becki had to admit, "We weren't super tight." Right away her mind flew to Gina saying that she was having a hard time connecting with coworkers. *Please tell me that I was more open to friendship with Louisa than Gina's coworkers are with her.*

"I do know that she lived alone. She told me she had a cleaning lady to help with the upkeep. I also know that Louisa had taste, I mean, look around you." Becki's hands opened to the room but she quickly dropped them. "Louisa paid for the kitchen job in one lump sum so she wasn't short of cash…"

"Did she discuss any other kind of problem she might be having?"

"No, she seemed quite content."

Karl was writing down notes in his pad as they conversed. All very official. Becki wondered if his questions varied in any way from the questions he would ask if she wasn't his wife. And if Gina wasn't their great friend. She'd never been interrogated by him at the scene of a murder before.

Yes, Gina had already indicated her suspicion that Louisa's death was deliberate.

Becki and Karl were a couple that talked in bed. She gabbed anyway. He responded appropriately. All the while at least one part of their bodies touched under the covers. A reassurance that the other was there. Tonight—this morning rather—she needed the comfort of that togetherness more than ever. From the moment she and Gina got home, until Karl crawled in beside her in the wee hours, Becki had kept herself pulled together as much as could be expected. But when Karl leaned over and kissed her in the darkness, tears welled up.

Karl took her in his arms. "I'm so sorry, Becki."

It was a wonder he understood her words between her sobs and hiccups and sniffs. Maybe he didn't. But it didn't matter because he was holding her and soothing her.

Eventually Becki felt her pulse calm and her breathing slow.

Karl smoothed her hair back and said, "You know, we weren't able to find any next of kin so we went ahead and released her name to the media."

Becki just listened now.

"Hon, there's a way you could help."

Oh, that was something she would like to do, if possible.

"I know you're busy with the shower and all," he continued, "but do you think there's any way you could go over to Louisa's house and just look through her things yourself with a woman's eye. See if there's something we missed. You're as detail-oriented as any of my men. Maybe more so. I'll tell everyone you're figuring out what charities to bring in and for which pieces. Otherwise, if no relatives turn up to make a claim, we'll just have to dump her stuff."

"Is this urgent, Karl? The shower's…" Gina came first after all.

"We don't put off for tomorrow what we can do today in crime investigation."

"Okay, I'll do it," she agreed reluctantly even though she couldn't imagine anything sadder than casual friends pawing through your things after you're dead and gone. "I'll bring Gina along if she doesn't object. She'll know what to do with clothes and jewelry and stuff like that."

Apparently satisfied, Karl rolled over.

Here we go, thought Becki, not really wanting to be left alone with images of her evening. *On top of that, Karl's snoring will start up like it does every night and I'll have to encase both ears in insulating pillow.*

When she and Karl married he didn't snore disruptively. Now it was loud snorts followed by long rattles followed by virtual roars. Maybe the variety depended on what Karl was dreaming about. Scientifically, she knew that with age the tissues in the throat loosen and vibrate. She'd complain more about it except that Karl never ever said a word about the tissues of her own body that were loosening and vibrating.

"Before you go to sleep, Karl…"

"Yes?" His muffled voice reached her from the far side of the bed.

"I'm worried about Gina too."

"Why is that?"

"She seems a bit down to me. Even before we found Louisa."

"Is she getting cold feet?"

"She says not."

"And you don't believe her?"

"No, I believe her. Some of her worries are work-related. But could it be partly Tony too? What do you think of him?"

Karl turned. The whites of his teeth flashed in the moonlight that slanted in through the window. "Not the *what do you think of Tony* question mere weeks before the wedding and seconds before I fall asleep."

Becki felt like jabbing him with one of the least loose-fleshed and vibration-prone parts of her body but held the impulse in check. He was only trying to lighten the mood.

"Tony's got a temper," she pointed out.

Only one more day to go before the shower and Becki and Gina were hanging over the rail of an old, white and red launch touring the shoreline. They were sheltered from the relentless sun beneath an awning.

A heat wave had plunged Southern and Central Ontario into a situation of high risk for power-outage due to extensive use of air-conditioners. Becki chose to live without air conditioning. Most of the time she enjoyed living in sync with outdoor temperatures during the summer. But every now and then heat and humidity got to be unbearable in their apartment above the store, even with all the windows and blinds closed and all the fans on full blast. Thankfully they lived near the lake and could go for emergency dips.

That's fine for us, thought Becki, *but what about Gina and guests at the shower if it stays hot like this? I mean, we're going to have to move the shower to our place from Louisa's.*

Gina seemed unperturbed about the change of venue and about the heat as well. Not a trace of sweat on her brow. "This is the first time I've seen Black Currant Bay from the point of view of the bay," she said.

"Pretty, isn't it?"

"Perfect," said Gina. "If I were a painter…"

Black Currant Bay and its surroundings really were inspirational and Becki was in no way blasé about her environment, but she knew that appearances can occasionally be deceiving.

Might as well get it over with, she thought. "Gina," she began, "when we get back in, there's something I have to do. You're welcome to join me, and in fact your presence would be helpful, but please don't feel obliged."

Gina cocked her head. "That sounds ominous…"

Becki gritted her teeth and shrugged. "Karl wants me to go through Louisa's house, look for any information that might lead to family members. Keep my eyes open for a clue as to what led to her death. Start thinking about packing her things. I told him I'd ask you to lend a hand."

Gina's eyebrows rose. "Oh, now he wants our help? I'm remembering what he told us at Louisa's. That it didn't look good that we turned up at the scene of a crime. I guess this latest request means we're only suspects on paper then?"

"Of course we're not suspects in Karl's eyes!"

Then Becki sighed. "Gina, this is not what I hoped for on your shower weekend. This and the heat!"

As she swiped a hand across her forehead, she noticed something peculiar. She pulled the binoculars that were hanging from a strap around her neck up to her eyes and scanned the shore.

"Hey! That's Louisa's house right there!" she said pointing.

"Where?"

"See the stone work and the lawn cascading down to the water?"

She played with the focus wheel to zoom in.

Her indignation must have shown.

"What?"

"There's a man skulking around. I think he's trying to get in."

Chapter 6

Becki borrowed Gina's cellphone to call Karl.

Gina didn't try to listen in. The sound of their conversation couldn't compete with the noise of the boat.

As Becki clicked off, Gina watched her forehead crease to a frown.

"He's sending a man over to check. We're to wait thirty minutes before going over there."

Gina nodded. "After we get back to land, let's walk over to her place. I could use the exercise." It was hot, but Gina didn't mind heat. She figured this was one of the advantages of being part Italian. Half her genes had originated in the sizzling Sicilian desert climate.

Now winter…that was a different story. Becki had a much greater tolerance for cold weather. And it sure got cold in this town, compared to Toronto.

Enjoy it now, Gina thought. She welcomed the sun on her face.

When they got to Louisa's house, Karl was waiting for them on the front porch.

"I have a man checking inside and we've done a full search of the grounds. Nothing appears to be forced. It's safe to go in."

Gina gulped.

"You still want us to try to find some clue as to her background?"

Karl didn't smile. This was business and his face was set to a determined look. "Anything you can find about where she may have come from before her life in Black Currant Bay will be helpful. We tried to follow up through the bank. They have a record of her opening an account in 1994, but no one remembers where she came from."

"She didn't have any papers or a safety deposit box?" These were such obvious questions, Gina felt silly for asking them.

"Not at this bank. We didn't find a safety deposit box key for anyplace else."

Weird, thought Gina.

"But she had a will," Becki said.

"Yes, a recent one with a local lawyer. But everything in it was local. No links to anyone outside of this town, and the lawyer doesn't know anything about her past."

Even weirder, thought Gina. *It's like the woman didn't exist before 1994.*

Becki sighed. "That's the problem with Canadians. We're too polite to pressure someone into telling us about their past."

"I'll leave you to it then," Karl said. He turned to Becki and his face softened. "See you at home about seven."

She nodded but didn't move to kiss him. *Not while he's on duty,* Gina noted, smiling.

Everything about Becki made her smile. *It's like she's a time capsule of everything that's good in the world.*

Karl left, and Gina followed Becki into the foyer.

Even though the house was hot, Gina was feeling a distinct chill. Memory of yesterday's discovery invaded her mind. She shook her head and followed Becki up the stairs.

This is kind of creepy, she thought, *going through a dead woman's closet.*

She'd never had to pack up a house after a death before. Anna and Becki had done it for Grandma, thank God.

"This is not going to be fun," she muttered to Becki.

"No, but it's important. Karl has a gut feel that his people may have missed something. They've already been through it all, so it's not as if we're disturbing a crime scene. Anything we can find that might give a clue to her past is useful."

They were in the second floor bedroom of the Victorian house. Even Gina had to admit that although it was old, the place was delightful. It had been beautifully restored, with gleaming hardwood floors and period furniture.

The bedroom was painted cream. Caramel and cream linens dressed the bed. A comfortable reading chair sat by the window, next to a small bookshelf.

The bed had been made with dainty throw cushions placed carefully at the head. This was obviously a woman who took pleasure in making things look nice.

Gina watched as Becki opened the antique dresser drawers, and carefully lifted each piece of delicate clothing.

"That's not the way to do it," Gina said. She went over and took a drawer right out and dumped it on the four-poster bed. "Much quicker. We're going to be giving these things to Goodwill, so it doesn't matter if they get a little wrinkled. Besides, then we can check the drawer bottoms to see if there's anything taped to them, like in the movies."

Becki frowned at the mess Gina was creating on the bed. "I'm sure Karl's people would have found anything like that."

Gina didn't miss Becki's expression. She smiled to herself. Becki was careful of everything, including feelings. That's one of the things that made her so pleasant to be around. "Well, why don't you do the dresser drawers, and I'll do the closet."

Gina marched over to the closet and opened the door.

Pretty ordinary stuff in there. She pawed through hangers. One serviceable all-purpose black dress with a V neck. A few summer dresses, pretty plain. Lots of pants with elastic waists on hangers. Longer skirts. Several fleece jackets. A velour housecoat that had seen better days.

She didn't bother to check pockets. Surely the cops had done that.

On the shelf above were purses and shoe boxes, lined up in a row. Nothing too special. A few good quality pumps, but certainly not designer. Two pairs of Mephisto sandals for summer. The purses were good-quality leather but plain, in uninspiring colours like navy and beige. She took each one down to look inside. Nothing. Not even a single tissue. This lady was truly abstemious.

"Find anything?" she asked Becki.

"Not really. Her underthings are pretty ordinary. No lover in the picture, I would guess."

Gina smiled. It seemed freaky that Becki would even think of a 'lover.'

"I'm going to check the other bedroom. She probably has older stuff stashed away in the closet there." *We all do*, Gina thought. *That's the whole reason for second bedrooms. Of course, if we built closets big enough in the first place…*

The guest bedroom was painted a pretty peach colour. The bed was sleekly furnished with good quality sheets and duvet in light grey. One night table held a reading lamp and small pile of books.

She walked to the closet and opened the door.

"Wow, oh wow," she murmured.

This was a magic closet. As a young girl, Gina would have gone mad for the clothes in there.

"Hey Becki, come here. You won't believe this."

Becki poked her brown head around the corner. Gina signalled her into the room.

"Look at this," she said. Her hands went into the closet and came out with a purple sequin evening gown with heavily padded shoulders. "Genuine late 80s couture wear, I'd bet my last dollar. The sort of thing you'd wear to a gala like the Brazilian Ball."

"Is it real, do you think?" Becki reached for it. "Wow, is it ever heavy."

"I know. I hate wearing sequin dresses. They kill your shoulders, and the sequins scratch your underarms." She looked in the neck for a tag. "Escher. Went out of business in the last recession, but man, at one time they were the cream of Bloor Street. That must have cost a bundle. At least two thousand. Back then, that was a lot."

Becki put it down on the bed and stepped back to admire it. "Wonder where she got it and why she had it?"

Gina was back in the closet, eagerly plowing through hangers. "A genuine lavender mink from Sellers-Gough. Holy cow, Becki, this is top drawer. And here's another evening gown."

She held up a black satin strapless gown with a huge sapphire blue bow at the back. "Clotheslines, I'll bet, from the late 80s. Yup, here's the tag. It is. They're out of business too."

"How do you know all this?" Becki asked, incredulously.

Gina grinned. "Mom always got *Vogue* magazine. Since before I could read, I would drool over it every month. These clothes were in style when I was a little kid. Big shoulders, lots of sequins…flashy colours and satin bows…you can imagine how I would react. It was the era of bling. And this," she pointed to the purple gown, "was the epitome of glamour."

Becki shook her head. "I never had anything like this."

"Most people wouldn't have a place to wear something like this." Gina picked up the gown and held it against her body. "That's the sort of number you could only wear at a major gala. Things like hospital fund-raisers and opera or symphony balls. When I got older, I read the Style section of *The Globe* every weekend." *Not to mention the society column.* She placed the gown reverently down on the bed.

All the Toronto elite went to the Brazilian Ball back then. Such a shame it no longer existed.

Whoa. Gina turned with a start. "Becki, how long have you known this woman?"

Becki squinted. "Since about a week after I got here. Eleven years ago. Louisa was not exactly friendly, but pleasant."

"What do you mean by that?"

"Well, she didn't invite me over here or anything. I got the impression she was a loner. But after a few months, she'd come sit beside me at functions and meetings." Becki looked thoughtful. "I liked her. She was never mean. Didn't say a bad thing about anyone. Always donated a decent amount to causes and stuff."

"Did you ever see her wear any of these things?"

Becki shook her head. "Nothing flashy. She was actually pretty dowdy. You know…didn't bother to cover the grey in her hair. Wore lots of Tabi sportswear. She blended in pretty well up here. Nobody was jealous of her or anything."

Gina turned back to the closet. She could just imagine the cops going through this. 'A bunch of old party clothes,' they would say.

And yet, here was a treasure trove of haute couture from the late 80s and early 90s. While most people, cops included, would have no idea what they were looking at, some collectors would kill for these items.

No, that was absolutely the wrong word. They wouldn't kill for clothes. Nobody would do that.

But it surely begged the question—how and why did these things end up here, hidden away in an old closet?

Easy. Gina could answer that, all right, because she would have done the same thing herself. It was as natural to her as breathing.

The woman couldn't bear to part with them.

Gina turned back to the closet. There were several less flashy day dresses and jackets. She quickly went through the labels—Holt Renfrew Signature, Creeds, Pat McDonagh, Marilyn Brooks, Linda Lundstrum and Bill Blass. Mainly Toronto designers, with a few New York celebrities thrown in.

Gina could imagine the woman standing in front of the closet, fingering the gorgeous materials and maybe even trying the items on one by one. Looking in the mirror…remembering her old life.

That was it, of course. This woman had a past. And it was one hell of a rich and glamorous one, probably in Toronto.

So why had she been living in disguise in the little town of Black Currant Bay?

Chapter 7

Becki and Karl had a busy day ahead of them. Today was Gina's wedding shower, and even in a small town, a Police Chief has plenty on his plate. Add murder and you have a recipe for mayhem.

He walked into their bedroom with a towel wrapped around his waist. *Now's the time to ask him,* thought Becki.

"We didn't go into it much last night and I understand that you can't share everything—"

"But...?" Karl never liked a whole lot of preamble. He was a straight-to-the-point kind of guy.

"Did you figure out who that fellow was that we called you about yesterday?" Becki asked. "The one walking around Louisa's property."

"I told you that we searched the grounds, and of course, we gave the interior the all-clear for you."

"Yeah, you said when you got there the place was deserted."

"So, dead end." He was buttoning up his white shirt.

"But a man prowling Louisa's property does seem suspicious to you, right?"

He leaned over the bed and stared at her. "Uh...this interrogation from one of the official suspects in the case?"

"Get real," Becki said.

"I'm sure there's an innocent explanation for the guy you saw on Louisa's property that has nothing to do with her death," he said. Karl's voice sounded more than just morning gruff. Like he was discouraging her from continuing this line of conversation.

"Like what?" she asked.

"The kid next door lobs a softball into deceased neighbour Louisa's yard by mistake and asks his father to go find it for him and bring it back."

Becki caught on to something he said in his previous sentence.

"Ah-ha! You said *death*. 'Louisa's death.' Why didn't you use the word *murder*? Are you purposely trying to play it down?"

"Standard police public relations advise us not to sensationalize crime." He slipped his belt through the loops of his pants.

"But Karl, you can't ask me to search for clues in a case and then completely downplay the event and...and...stonewall me about the details."

"I can't?"

"No, you can't. It's against the rules."

"What rules?"

"Marriage rules."

Karl lifted his eyebrows twice in quick succession. His equivalent to a wink. "New marriage rules get added a decade later?"

Becki rolled her eyes. "Look, thanks to Gina and me, you have a new avenue of investigation in the case. One which may or may not help you find next of kin and/or a motive for Louisa's murder."

"The fancy frocks?"

"Louisa obviously had some kind of a fashionable life in the past, before she came up here to Black Currant Bay."

"You're bargaining for something, aren't you? I can hear it in your voice."

"The least you can do is tell me why you've labelled Louisa's death a crime. Kind of a waste of time for Gina and I to keep our eyes peeled if we don't know what we're keeping our eyes peeled for."

"Okay, this is just between you and me."

"And Gina."

He paused.

"And she'll probably tell Tony," Becki added.

"Is that all?"

"I'm sure that's it."

"Well, I'm afraid to say that you're right. Your former client Louisa was intentionally sent toppling to her death."

For a brief moment Becki felt like she couldn't breathe. Although at this point it was ridiculous to hope for a less than malicious cause of death, she found herself asking, "So, for sure, Louisa couldn't have just fallen?"

"She was battered and cut," Karl said. "It looks like more than from a fall down the stairs. And there was a chair down there too. A chair smeared with blood."

The vision of Louisa crumpled at the bottom of her own staircase was one Becki was never going to be able to delete from her memory, and knowing that someone purposely sent the poor woman down to the cold hard cement made it so much worse.

Luckily she had a lot of last-minute shower preparations to do, which would distract her for a while.

She sent Gina off for a morning at the beach. She lent her a sun umbrella to stick in the sand to protect her from the blazing rays. It was going to be a scorcher of a day. Thankfully, the threat of intolerable humidity seemed to be holding off. The festivities could go on as anticipated and none of the guests, not to mention the bride-to-be, would drown in sweat.

She made sure to tell Gina not to overindulge in chocolate malteds. There would be mountains of food for everyone to share this afternoon.

She wondered who would arrive first carrying a present and/or a platter. Anne wouldn't be attending at all because she was holding down the fort at the store, and of the two great friends Becki'd made since coming to Black Currant Bay, only Kathleen could come today. France was on holiday visiting relatives in Québec.

The rest of the guests would be an assortment of townsfolk—clients of hers, fellow shopkeepers—all of whom had either met Gina during one of her many visits here, or finagled an invitation because they loved Gina on TV.

Gina was a celebrity. The local *Black Currant Bay Beacon Star* had gotten wind of the shower and planned to send a cameraman.

There had already been coverage in Toronto of Gina's prenuptials. Gina had attended many other parties thrown by relatives and friends that Becki didn't even know about. But the more celebrations the merrier in her opinion. Most importantly, she wanted to count herself among the folks to have offered Gina an old-fashioned circle of love—the company of women of all ages to wish her well on her journey of commitment *until death do us part.*

"Oh my God! It's gorgeous!" cried Becki, once she saw the dress, which Gina extricated from its protective garment bag.

"Stunning!" all the others agreed.

"A Vera Wang original." Gina beamed at the centre of it all and swished her wedding dress around on its padded hanger to show off the back.

Of course! thought Becki. *The back of a wedding gown has to be just as eye-popping as the front. During the ceremony the bride is, in fact, viewed longer from behind than she is from the front.*

Gina's wedding gown was cut from the very best silk into a strapless mermaid shape. Gina's voluptuous curves would fill it spectacularly. And as if Gina's perfect complexion wouldn't glow with pure happiness enough to dim the ceremonial candles in the church on the day of her wedding, hand-sewn into the intricate lace overlay of the skirt and its short train were thousands of Swarovski crystals.

A dozen more flashes went off. Becki pictured the resulting photo and accompanying caption in her mind.

Weather Network's Gina Monroe unveils her wedding gown at a private shower in Black Currant Bay.

Would Gina really give permission to the local paper to print such a shot? Becki worried it would leak to the national papers. To the Internet. Mostly she worried the groom would see the bride's dress before their wedding day. Very, very bad luck. Everyone knew that.

Chapter 8

"A fondue pot! How retro! I love it." Gina didn't love it, but she would never let this elderly lady know that. What was her name? Lottie. Short for Charlotte, no doubt.

Lottie smiled back. Her medium length white hair was speckled with grey, and hung in unruly waves. She was dressed in all maroon Tabi. *And therefore her best clothes.* Gina had to smile. She looked down and flicked a piece of lint off her own designer shift dress in dazzling shades of green and blue.

"I'm so glad you like it," Lottie bubbled. "Mason's had it on sale, and I was so lucky to get it at that price."

Someone snorted.

"What?" said Lottie. "Oh. I guess I shouldn't have mentioned that?" She looked like a stricken Miss Marple.

"It's smart to get things on sale," Becki said kindly. "Especially when giving a gift. You can buy so much more."

Lottie perked up. "That's what I thought. I was going to ask Louisa to go in with me, but then she—oh." Lottie fell silent, as did the room.

Talk about the Elephant in the room. You just couldn't ignore it, so Gina nodded sympathetically. "I'm so sorry. Did you know her well?"

Lottie nodded. She seemed to be holding back tears. "She was my best friend."

People in the room shuffled uncomfortably. Voices dropped to murmurs.

Gina sighed. She patted Lottie's shoulder, not knowing how much to say. The police hadn't let slip that Louisa's death was anything other than an accident. Most people just thought she had lost her footing and fallen down the stairs.

Still, it certainly put a damper on this shower that the poor lady was supposed to have co-hosted.

"More coffee?" Becki stood before her with the pot in her hand, ready to refill.

Gina smiled her thanks. Typical of Becki to move to action when there was an awkward moment.

As Becki moved over to fill Lottie's cup, Gina sat back to watch the others.

It was natural to be sad when a neighbour died. All these women seemed to be covering up their feelings of discomfort by being overly cheerful. Yet Gina noticed one thing.

Lottie seemed to be the only person who seemed truly distraught that Louisa had died.

When Becki moved on, Lottie turned to her.

"I'm so glad Becki went ahead with this," Lottie said in a low voice. "Really, I think Louisa would have wanted it." She nodded vigorously.

Why do people always say that? Who knows what the dead would have wanted? Probably they had other, more important things on their minds now...

"I offered to move the shower to my place, but it really is too tiny."

Gina smiled and inclined her head.

Poor Becki. She had planned this shower for weeks, inviting all her Black Currant friends. Mary, Pat, Lottie, Joan, Kathleen...and three other women whose names she couldn't remember. All nice. All kind of old. Well, Becki was the youngest of them, and she was at least fifty. There didn't seem to be many young women left in small towns. No jobs, she supposed.

But you had to admire them. These generous women had all brought presents and had gone to town with baking. Becki's charming living room bloomed with cheery cut flowers displayed in the several cut glass and ceramic vases.

And now there was a definite grey feeling hanging in the air, like chilly drizzle. *Shower...drizzle. It was peculiarly ironic.*

She tried to shake herself free of it. Up to her to rescue the party and make others feel comfortable. Later, she would corner Lottie to learn more about the murder victim.

Gina's smile lit up the room. She addressed the group. "I can't tell you how much I appreciate all you've done for this shower. Everyone has been so kind. It's just not like this in Toronto. People are different."

That was exactly the right thing to say to get everyone nodding and talking. Gina smiled to herself.

"I've always said that about cities," sniffed Mary, the reverend's thin wife. "Couldn't pay me to live there."

"They don't even say hello on the streets!" the woman in the flowered dress piped up.

"Not even the shopkeepers." Well-dressed Pat owned the only women's clothing shop in town. *Probably where Lottie had gotten the Tabi ensemble.*

"You're very lucky to live here. I wish I could," Gina said.

She looked around the room. Everyone seemed pleased.

It was only a little bit of a lie. Gina had to live near Toronto for her work at The Weather Network. But Tony was building them a lovely home in the country, in Caledon, one of the outer suburbs. She really was looking forward to leaving the noise of the city. *Or course, as long as one was close enough to drive in for the restaurants and shopping...*

Becki plopped another carefully wrapped present in her lap. "Here, open this one next."

Gina peeled back the tape, as directed.

"A salad spinner! Just what I need." It could join the other three in her condo.

When the gifts were all opened and proudly displayed on the dining nook table, everyone milled cheerfully around the kitchen counter, plopping little goodies onto their vintage plates. Homemade pickles, finger sandwiches, squares of every size and make...lemon, date, brownies, something called 'Sex in a Pan' which made everyone giggle, especially the older ladies. Truly, this was a luscious escape from the diet world.

Gina made some careful choices, always conscious of the camera and her figure, but still indulging herself. She turned to see where Lottie had gone to and found the woman at her side. The little lady's head barely came up to her shoulders.

"Will you sit with me?" Lottie's voice was shaky. "I'm a little lost without my friend here." She looked at Gina with something like hero-worship.

"Of course," Gina said. "It's lovely on the back deck. Shall we go there?"

Gina led the way out the kitchen door. Becki's balcony was always a delight at this time of year. Colourful blooms made the air fragrant all about them.

There were two Muskoka chairs set up a little away from the patio table and chairs. She headed for the blue chair and sat down.

"I love to watch you on The Weather Network. It's so much fun to know someone famous."

Gina never knew how to respond when people said things like that. It wasn't as if she were a movie star. So usually, she just mumbled, "Thank you."

"Do they give you all those lovely clothes?"

Now she was back on familiar ground. "Most of them are my own. But sometimes certain shop owners will give me things to wear on the air, just to get their names listed in the credits. I'm always grateful."

Lottie sighed. "So where are you going on your honeymoon?"

The voice was eager. This woman probably spent a lot of time living vicariously through others, Gina thought.

"A week in London and Paris," she said.

"Oh!" The old lady clapped her hands together. "I was born in England! I've always wanted to go back there. Are you going to Cornwall?"

Gina shook her head. "Not this trip. There isn't time." She took a bite from an egg and tuna finger sandwich.

"I'm from Cornwall," Lottie said wistfully. "We moved when I was five. I still remember parts of it. The little stone cottages with climbing roses. The palm trees along the shore."

"It sounds beautiful."

"It was. There was something magical about it. Louisa and I used to talk about travelling there. We were going to go together and share a room. But I guess I won't be going there now." Sadness flowed from her.

Gina didn't know what to say. "I'm sorry. Is there anyone else you could go with?"

Lottie shook her head. "I wouldn't have the money. Louisa was going to pay for our room."

Gina continued to munch. She realized it must be hard to live on a meagre pension. She should ask Becki about this woman's circumstances. Maybe there was something she and Tony could do.

"There are ghosts in Cornwall," Lottie said. Her voice had changed. The chatter had morphed to something dreamy with a hint of darkness.

Gina's head shot up. "How do you know?"

"I saw them." Lottie's head bobbed up and down. "When I was a little girl."

Gina smiled down at her plate. Lottie was an odd duck. Did it come from living alone for so long?

"A beautiful lady in white, and a young man on a horse. Her dress was long and flowing, like they used to wear in the olden days. They would meet in the fields behind our cottage at night."

Gina listened indulgently.

"Of course, I don't know if the dress was really white. Everything about ghosts seems to be black and white, have you noticed? Like an old

TV. There's never any color. I wonder if it's because they're old, or because they're dead."

Still one sweet left. Gina popped it into her mouth.

"And of course, they speak to me now."

Crackers, thought Gina. *She hears voices in her head. They have a name for that.*

Lottie leaned forward and lowered her voice. "You should always listen to ghosts. It's not safe to ignore them."

When Gina went to get coffee from the big metal carafe, Mary, the reverend's wife came up to her side.

"Was Lottie boring you with her talk of Cornwall? She does go on and on about it."

Gina reached for cream. *Real cream, bless Becki's heart.* She poured it into her coffee.

"That. But mainly, she was talking of ghosts."

Mary snorted. "Don't pay any attention to her. Lottie has a screw loose. Still, it was good of you to humour her. Most people find her…trying."

"What are you trying? Something exciting?" As usual, Becki's timing was perfect.

"I'm trying to resist any more of these goodies. I'm going to be a fat pig for my wedding if I stay another week with you, Becki." Gina patted her tummy.

"I'll bet that pretty dress won't fit you a year from now," Becki quipped. "Maybe I'll be hosting a different kind of shower?"

Laughter tinkled.

"Becki, she's going to kill you!" Pat made a knife across the throat motion with her hand.

Gina shivered.

Chapter 9

Gina smiled through the flash of the camera like the pro she was. The young male photographer winked at her, then moved away quickly.

"I'm sorry about this," Becki said ruefully. "I thought the shower would be enough."

"Damned reporters have to follow you all over town," grumbled Karl. "Can't even have a decent meal out without the vultures gathering."

He grimaced suddenly.

Gina held back a giggle. Becki had obviously kicked him under the table.

"Thanks for being such a good sport," Becki said. "It's just that you're famous in this town. Isn't often we get a celebrity here."

"Oh, I don't mind." Gina smiled. At least she was looking good today. Her hair was behaving. The flapper-style silk slip dress was perfect for dining at Pastas on a warm humid night.

"And thanks again for insisting on taking us out here," Becki continued. "I adore this place, and it's like pulling teeth to get Karl to move from the kitchen at home."

"That's because you're the best cook around," Karl said.

Becki beamed. *Smart man*, Gina thought.

"It's my pleasure hosting tonight. You were wonderful to give me that shower. I enjoyed it a lot. And Becki, remember all those times you treated me when I was a kid? I used to love coming to stay. Still do. You can't imagine the pleasure it gives me to be able to reciprocate now that I am in a position to do so."

Karl grunted. He always seemed pleased when Becki was praised.

Tonight, the air was resplendent with odours of tomato, basil and sweet garlic. *Yum. Good thing this dress had no waistline. Those girls in the 1920s knew how to party.*

"Lovely place," she said, gazing around the room. "Whimsical without being overdone. It truly looks like a bistro in Italy." She picked up the black leather menu folder and opened it.

"Grub's good too," Karl stated.

"Oh for goodness sake, Karl!"

Gina had to smile. Becki was always scolding Karl with affection. She knew he loved it. In fact, she was sure he egged Becki on by artfully planting little male-isms like this last one. Probably Becki was on to him, but that was part of the fun.

They had the best relationship of any married couple she knew.

Would she and Tony be so happy?

The waiter brought a tray of water goblets and a basket of crusty rolls. She looked at them longingly.

"What do you have to do to get some wine around here?" Karl asked.

"*Karl!*" Becki scolded. She shook her head.

Gina laughed. "My treat tonight, so I'm ordering what I want. That okay?"

She turned to the waiter. "A bottle of Amarone and a good Pinot Grigio, please."

Becki gasped. "Gina! That's too much."

"Nonsense. This is a special occasion. Karl, do you want a cocktail to start?"

He shook his head. Gina could see him smiling behind the menu. They were co-conspirators tonight, as usual. It was such fun to tease Becki.

"Three glasses," she said to the waiter. He smiled and walked away.

"What do you recommend, Becki? I had the gnocchi last time. It was great, but I want to try something else."

"I love the linguine with mushrooms, parsley and parmesan."

"Sold," said Gina. She snapped the menu shut and placed it down on the starched white tablecloth. "And Caesar salad." Light on the dressing, of course. This weekend had put at least one pound on her, already.

Karl was helping himself to a crusty white roll. She gathered her thoughts to help her resist temptation.

"So. About Louisa. I'm thinking I could do a little research in Toronto among my society contacts. Ask around, see if anyone from their crowd went missing two decades ago. Is that okay with you, Karl?"

"Let me think," he said. "You'd have to be subtle. Don't want you stirring anything up that could put you in danger."

It was funny even hearing Karl use the word 'subtle.' It was even funnier thinking of these front page society matrons as dangerous. *Unless you considered perfectly groomed fake fingernails a weapon.*

"Thing is," Gina continued, "I know a few women who were in that high society clique many years ago. Friends of Mom's. I can ask them individually over lunch."

"What excuse would you have for asking them, Gina?"

Good question. Becki was always a quick thinker.

"Maybe something along fashion lines. I could say I'm doing a segment on Toronto designers of the 80s and 90s, for the Life Network. I came across a few photos, and I can identify most of the women, but there was one wearing Pat McDonagh who I'd like to get in touch with for an interview."

Karl looked sceptical. "Do people really care about that crap?"

"*Karl*!"

Gina smiled. "Let me start with Mom. She might have some ideas. I'll get her to invite them out for lunch, one by one."

Becki groaned. "Gina, you'll never fit into your dress by the wedding."

"Salad and wine, Becki. Salad and wine. Those women are allergic to carbs."

At the sound of the word, temptation won out. Gina's slim hand reached across the table for a crusty white roll.

Next morning, when she was packing up her suitcase, doubts crept into Gina's mind.

Becki sat on the edge of the bed, looking sad.

"Are you sure you have to go already? You could stay here a few more days. Karl would be delighted."

Gina looked up. "I'd love to but I can't."

It was true too. She did love Black Currant Bay—the quiet town, the quirky houses and the gentle, eccentric people up here. Of course, they would probably consider themselves normal, and city people eccentric.

Becki looked down at her hands. "It's just that this must be what empty nest syndrome feels like. I get used to you being here, and then you leave."

Now she laughed. "Becki, I'm coming back up in just two months. And you know you can always come down to the city anytime to stay with me."

"Hate the city," Becki grumbled.

"Then good thing I'm moving to the country with Tony. You'll enjoy visiting there."

Gina smiled. It felt good to be missed by Becki. She closed the top of the suitcase and zipped it up.

"Besides, the wedding is almost here. You're coming down for that."

Becki brightened. "I have that new dress for it. Can't wait to pick it up at the store."

Gina moved out the hall to the adjacent bathroom. She gathered up her makeup bag and carried it back to the guest bedroom.

"What do you really think about Louisa, Becki? Do you think we'll be able to find out who she really was?"

Becki pushed off the bed, then immediately turned around and smoothed the bedcover with her hands.

"I think it's really hard to hide from someone who is determined to find you. But she's done it all these years and got away with it until this week. So my question is, 'what happened recently to 'blow her cover,' as they say in the movies?'"

"You mean, something has come to light recently. Something that pointed to her location and spooked the killer to act."

Becki paused at the door. "It could be that. Or it could be that someone has been out of circulation for twenty years, and has just gotten free."

Gina started. "You mean like prison?"

Becki cocked her head. "That's one possibility. I can think of other places too."

A pause.

"Be careful, Gina. I'm getting a bad feeling about this."

"You aren't suggesting we let this go, are you?"

Becki shook her head. "We have to try to do something. The fact that we discovered her body makes us suspects, whatever Karl says."

"Then her killer must be found. I don't want this hanging over my head." So far, Karl had managed to keep this out of the Toronto papers. But it was only a matter of time.

"I'm planning to do a little sleuthing from my end," said Becki. "We just both need to be careful. Let Tony know what you're doing, and where you are at all times."

Gina pulled the suitcase off the bed to the floor. "The last part should be easy. But I'm not looking forward to telling him what we're doing."

Chapter 10

From: Gina Monroe
Sent: June-10-14 7:15 AM
To: Rebekkah Green
Subject: LOVED IT!

Hi Becki,

That was fun! I loved spending time with you and Karl and I loved, loved, loved the shower you threw me! What a great way to kick off the summer! I miss you and Black Currant Bay already. Look forward to seeing you again in just a little over 2 weeks!

Thanks again,

XO Gina

From: Rebekkah Green
Sent: June-10-14 2:30 PM
To: Gina Monroe
Subject: YOU ARE SOOO WELCOME

Hi Gina,

Totally my pleasure throwing that little shindig! I had fun too. I have to tell you that guests have been commenting about how much they enjoyed your shower and I can tell by their expression that you have them completely under your spell. Forever fans.

How did Tony react when you told him you were going to try and find out more about Louisa through her stashed collection of designer clothes? I know you were imagining when you left here that he wouldn't be happy about it. I really hope you're wrong.

Thought you'd be interested to know that before I even started asking around about Louisa on this end, a tiny piece of the puzzle seems to have fallen into place on its own. Remember that guy we spotted on Louisa's property on Friday? Well, Saturday while you and I were partying it up, a man came into Beautiful Things and talked about hiring us down the road to decorate a sales centre/model home for a new waterfront development coming to town.

Anne, who you remember was minding the store, says this Douglas Spellman fellow has been buying up as many waterfront properties as he can get a hold of, all on the hush hush. His initial proposal to the Black Currant Bay Planning Board is for a community of 100 town homes. Get this. Each town home will be built above a boathouse. His spiel: *Small-town Black Currant Bay—Port to the World.*

According to him, new homeowners will have access to a private sandy beach, tennis courts… All very exclusive. He thinks he'll soon be at the pre-sell stage and is hoping to hire local firms such as ours for construction etc. in order to help with community relations. Gina, I'm telling you, it's the first I've heard of it.

Anyway, I'm betting it was Mr. Spellman we saw scouting Louisa's property. Probably figures a deceased person's land is easily negotiated. How does he even know Louisa lived on the waterfront?

Whoa, have I gotten off subject! A heartfelt "you're sooo welcome" to the loveliest bride-to-be in all of Ontario!

♥ Becki

PS Thanks for giving us a sneak peek of your wedding dress. I'm still dazzled!

From: Gina Monroe
Sent: June-12-14 7:18 AM
To: Rebekkah Green
Subject: TONY WAS NOT HAPPY

Hi Becki,

Tony said I should keep my nose out of things that are way out of my element. It's like he thinks I'm good for the weather and for looking good and for…well you know what men are always obsessed with…and that's it that's all. I am so pissed!

Okay. Calm down, Gina. I'm trying to get a hold of myself here as you can tell. The worst part of it is I was upfront with Tony—I believe in open, honest communication between partners after all—and yet here I am, and I haven't told you this yet, suspecting for a while now that Tony is not being honest and open with me.

Becki, you know that I'm intuitive. That I have a knack for interpreting signs, be they weather-related or not. That's why I'm sure I'll dig up something about Louisa by talking to clients and owners of some of the stores down here. That's also why I'm sure that Tony has secretly returned to his Canadian Security Intelligence Service job. After he promised he was happy working as an architect.

Trust.

It's the most important thing in a relationship. I bet Karl doesn't keep secrets from you.

XO Gina

From: Rebekkah Green
Sent: June-12-14 10:30 AM
To: Gina Monroe
Subject: TONY

Oh Gina,

I'm sorry you're upset and I feel responsible since it's me that got you involved in the Louisa thing in the first place.

Yes, Karl has kept secrets from me. I'm trying to train him never to do it again.

A man seems to think that what his partner doesn't know won't hurt. Often he won't talk about what's going on until whatever it is is over with, figuring that the end result is all that matters. In the meantime, his partner knows something's not right, and of course, she feels left out, unappreciated and imagines the worst.

Am I getting any of this right?

Hope you and Tony straighten this out. I know he loves you, Gina, and you love him too. If not, you wouldn't be so angry right now.

Becki

Chapter 11

Tony didn't answer his phone when Gina called after work. He wasn't in the condo when Gina got home from the studio. She reread the hand-written note he had left on the black granite countertop. He'd obviously written it before he made the call to Black Currant.

Something came up. Have to catch a plane. Call you when I can. Sorry.

It was the 'sorry' that gave it away. Gina was pretty sure he had never said 'sorry' in his entire life.

This meant he was doing something he shouldn't be. And Gina had a pretty good idea what that would be.

Yup, he was feeling plenty guilty, all right.

Gina dropped her keys on the counter. She threw her purse on the bar stool, kicked off her Manolo heels and then walked over to the floor to ceiling windows.

The city looked grey tonight. Twilight was being masked by thin clouds. Still, the lights of the city underneath the clouds were starting to twinkle.

It did little to soothe her frustration. And yes, if she were being honest, her fear.

For if there was one thing that scared Gina above everything else, it was Tony going back to his old job. The one nobody talked about. The one he had promised to give up.

Good thing she was fully occupied for the next few days. Tomorrow was a full day of work. And Saturday, she would have lunch with two of the women from her mother's hospital charity committee.

In the meantime, she would try to find out where Tony had gone.

The Bloor Street Diner was a fixture in Toronto. In the 80s, it had been a hip black and pink resto located on the second floor beside Holt Renfrew, that bastion of retail couture. Some years ago, it moved across the street to the Manulife Centre, where it continued its career as a lunch spot for the movers and shakers in the city, and their well-heeled wives.

Gina was the last to arrive. She saw her mother Anna seated at a black granite-topped table with two other slender women, and waved.

As she walked over to the table, she smiled to herself. These women made her own smart mother look small town. Of course, they were a few years younger than her mom, she figured.

Still, Gina was glad she had chosen to wear the new Prada dress today.

She slid gracefully into the sleek chair and smiled her greeting.

Gina had met these women before, of course. You couldn't be a local television celebrity and not get invited to all the charity functions in town.

Delia was a natural blonde, and seemed slimmer than ever. Her face looked good though. Work obviously done there.

Cathy was a little more rounded, but still in good shape. Her caramel hair was shorter but perfectly cut to the shape of her head in a tumble of curls.

"I was just telling the girls about that photo, Gina. Have you got it with you?" Gina's mother said.

Gina reached into her portfolio purse and pulled out the photo of Louisa taken up north last summer.

"This is the woman we're trying to find the name of," she said.

Cathy took it from her fingers. She squinted at it, then cursed. Next, she reached into her Gucci purse to retrieve reading glasses.

Not just any reading glasses, of course. Christian Dior. Gina watched as Cathy perched them on her nose and peered down at the photo.

A pause.

"Nope. Don't know her," said Cathy. She passed the photo to Delia.

The second woman gazed at the photo for some time. "Hand me your glasses," she said to Cathy.

"You should get your own." Cathy grumbled, but handed over her specs.

"I have my own. They just don't fit in this purse, with my sunglasses."

Gina had to smile. A lipstick and credit card would fill most of that tiny Kate Spade clutch.

Delia stared at the photo for several seconds.

"Cath, take a peek at this again. Imagine her twenty-five years younger, as a blonde."

Cathy took back the glasses and the photo. "Oh. You're thinking, the chin?"

Gina peered at the photo. It was true. Louisa had a sweetheart-shaped face with a gently pointed chin.

Delia nodded. "Remember that wife of the guy who was charged with embezzlement? The entertainment guy? *You* know."

Gina's mother looked excited. "I know who you mean! She used to hang out with the older girls on the charity circuit—you know, the Brazilian Ball belles. What was her name?"

"There was Anna-Maria...Catherine...I can't remember the other one."

"She used to wear Oscar de la Renta," Delia mused. "And Clotheslines. I remember she had this fabulous gown, black satin strapless, with a huge blue bow on the back. Very late 80s. I tried to get it for the St. Andrew's Ball, but they wouldn't do two of them."

Gina felt her blood rise. The Clotheslines gown that had been in the closet in Black Currant Bay! It had to be the same one.

Finally—a solid lead to her identity!

Now, if they could only remember her name. But it wouldn't be too hard to find out. The entertainment guy, who went down for embezzlement, shouldn't be difficult to dig up. She could call her newspaper contacts. See if they could search the file stories to come up with the name.

Did they have computer files back in the late 80s? Maybe not. Maybe it would have to be an in-person search.

What did they call that old stuff...microfilm?

Delia reached for the photo again. "Gad, what the march of time will do to you if you don't have the proper services." She shivered.

Services, meaning Botox, proper hair salons and hot young personal trainers, Gina thought wryly. Louisa had let natural aging take place. These women wouldn't admire her for that.

"So what happened to her husband? Didn't he get convicted?" Delia said to Cathy. Her face had a funny look on it.

"I read he was connected to the mob," Cathy said, fiddling with her purse. "But they were several years older than us, so we weren't in their clique."

"I can't remember what became of her. She sort of faded from view," Gina's mother said.

"It was worse than that," Delia said, pursing her Dior-red lips. Her forehead should have wrinkled, but of course, it didn't. "Society can be cruel. Sort of like in the olden days. If you had a scandal in the family, you never got invited anywhere again."

"So you're saying this woman would have become a pariah because of her husband?" Gina asked. The pieces were beginning to fit together. Husband going to prison. All the money gone. Friends jumping from a sinking ship. Maybe even the mob involved.

"I'm sorry, sweetie. I didn't know her personally. But it sounds logical," Anna said.

"Those high society matrons can be such bitches," Delia said.

Gina watched her mother smother a smile.

"It was all such a long time ago," Cathy said. "So much has happened since then. All the Toronto high flyers are different. Why are you trying to track her down, anyway?"

Gina hesitated. She didn't know if this should be common knowledge, or something she should keep secret. So she hedged just a teeny bit.

"The woman in the photo died up north. People are trying to track down the family."

Delia brushed her platinum hair back behind her ear. One large diamond winked on her earlobe. "There wouldn't be much money in it. The guy went bankrupt, for sure."

Anna frowned. "Not everything is about money, Del."

"You bet your sweet ass it is, honey. Don't let anyone tell you different, Gina."

The smarmy waiter returned with lunch plates. Four green salads with fresh berries, avocado, and dressing on the side, plus another bottle of white wine. Gina snuck a piece of Italian bread onto her plate. She didn't dare reach for a butter ball with all those eyes watching.

"So I hear you bought Vera Wang for the wedding dress," Cathy said.

Gina nodded. Her mouth was full.

"Here's something I don't understand," Delia said. "If you're already living together, how do you keep the groom from seeing the dress before the wedding?"

"We're not exactly living together yet," Gina said. "But Tony doesn't care much about clothes. He wouldn't bother to go looking. Besides, he's away right now, so it isn't a problem."

Gina's mother raised an eyebrow. "Why is he away, sweetheart? I thought all his clients were in town now."

Gina instantly realized her mistake. She couldn't tell them why Tony was away. She couldn't even tell them where he really was. She didn't know herself.

Her hesitation was a dead give-away.

The two women opposite exchanged glances. One looked away, awkwardly.

Delia sniffed. "My first husband cheated on me."

Gina started. "Tony isn't cheating on me. He's just away on business."

Cathy ran a manicured finger down the stem of her wine glass. "The only good thing about being cheated on is if you're married. Makes the divorce settlement richer."

Delia laughed. "So get yourself married to him, Gina. The sooner the better."

"Girls, don't be nasty. I'm sure Tony's not seeing anyone else. He's not the sort," Gina heard her mother say.

Delia snorted. "Anna, don't be naïve. They're *all* the sort."

"Not this one. If you could see him with Gina, you would know." Anna was firm.

For the umpteenth time in her life, Gina thanked God for giving her such a terrific mother.

Delia figured she'd done well to keep her mouth shut in the restaurant. That's what good friends were for. But now, in the car, she couldn't keep quiet.

"Why didn't you tell them his name?" she said to Cathy.

"Whose name?" Cathy's voice was barely a whisper.

"Come on, Cath! We've been friends for a long time. You wouldn't forget his name. Not him."

Cathy fiddled with the handles of her purse. "You're wrong, Del. I tried to forget everything. I really did."

Chapter 12

The information she had gleaned called for more than an e-mail. Gina dialled Becki at work.

"Beautiful Things," Becki responded.

"Hi, it's Gina. Have I caught you at a good time?"

"Any time's a good time for you."

"Really? Are there clients in the store?"

There was a pause while she assumed Becki took a quick look around.

"No. I'm all by myself here, struggling to eliminate items from this pile of ideas and samples that I've gathered around me. I'm searching for the best solution for the job we're working on." She sighed. "Not easy. How about you? You okay?"

"I guess. As you know, Tony is away on a trip." Gina thought about it, then admitted, "That conversation that Tony and I need to have about underestimating me will have to be had later in person." Then she hurried on because she didn't want to put Becki on the spot. "Guess what? I found out who Louisa is."

"Already?"

The surprise in Becki's voice was just a little bit unflattering, but Gina made light of it. "You know what they say, 'follow the clothes'."

"And where did they lead?"

"To an entertainment head honcho. One who apparently embezzled, who perhaps was connected to the mob, and who may have gone to jail."

"In-ter-est-ing…"

"This guy may be Louisa's husband, or her ex since the two of them were obviously separated for years."

"I can't picture it. Our quiet Louisa married to some sleazy showbiz mogul? Some guy who sits behind a great big chestnut desk with a matching built-in bookcase behind him. The furniture too heavy and the room dark. Signed black and white head shots the only frames on the wall and the wee bit of sparkle in the space coming from the decanter of whiskey on a side table—"

"I didn't realize you imagined people in terms of décor."

"Job hazard. You'd be surprised how connected people and their personal spaces are."

"People show their true selves without realizing it, don't they? For me it's the fashion angle."

"And yet Louisa appears to have hidden her true identity in Black Currant Bay for years."

"She must have been *trying* to fool people," Gina said. "Most of the time not wearing the beautiful garments she was accustomed to wear."

"Is her name really Louisa?"

"Good question. I'm not sure. I'm going to do some more digging. Just thought you'd like to know what I found out today. I suppose you need to pass it on to Karl."

"I should."

"I hear a 'but'."

"Do we know enough yet? Don't you want to wait until we can present him with a solid name for Louisa's next of kin? That's what we're supposed to be looking for."

"Sure, let's show Karl *and* Tony what we can do!"

"Being careful though," Becki warned. "I want you to know something about guys with big desks."

"Becki!"

"Ha! If they choose to take up more space than they need and it's all for effect, they may be trying to intimidate."

Now Becki had Gina's interest. "Honest to God? There's a relationship between desk size and behaviour?"

"Studies show that people who sit behind large desks are more likely to cheat, steal—"

"You're kidding, right?"

"No."

"How come I've never heard any of this?"

"Don't know. Anyway, large desk owners may start to feel that they're above the rules that govern lesser drones."

Gina was relieved that Becki couldn't see her eyes popping, but it seemed she gave herself away with some sort of non-verbal expression that Becki interpreted as a snicker.

"I'm not joking! The question is whether the power of an influential job, one that permits a swanky office and an impressive desk, is what corrupts, or if a pre-existing sense of entitlement lends itself to corruption, which then leads to a position of power and influence. It's a 'Which comes first, the chicken or the egg?' sort of thing."

"Well, at this point we're just presuming Louisa's husband has a big desk."

As soon as Gina hung up the phone, her momentary high from talking to Becki crashed. Thing is, when her primary relationship with Tony wasn't going perfectly, nothing seemed right with the world.

My God, was she becoming dependent? No way she wanted to be like that!

Maybe eating something—like supper—would make her feel better. She strolled into her kitchen.

There were no windows there, but because the condo was open concept she could still see out the wall of glass in the adjacent living room. In a couple hours the night sky would be at its blackest. Toronto's pattern of lights always reminded her of strings of vintage necklaces scattered on velvet.

What to eat?

She swung open cupboard doors and peeked here and there. She had to admit this condo had the snazziest kitchen. Sparkly granite countertops. Shiny stainless appliances. Rich hardwood cabinets.

But nothing to eat. At least nothing appealing.

Becki's cupboards on the other hand would be stocked with different shapes of pasta, lentils, couscous, flour, wild rice, olive oil, chocolate, herbal teas, exotic spices... Not to mention a few veggie things Gina might not be able to identify. Plus her refrigerator would be like a horn of plenty filled with fruit and vegetables.

Becki had a whole blog-full of vegetarian recipes online. She also had a husband to cook for, and he, being the smart little devil he was, knew enough to encourage her with praise to elicit all kinds of home cooked goodness.

It's not like I can't cook, Gina thought. *I'm Italian for heaven's sake! The big problem is who wants to cook for oneself?*

Then she straightened her spine, and in a tone that carried no small amount of reproach, pointed out to her invisible fiancé sitting on a barstool at the kitchen island, "Cooking for two is not a convincing enough reason to get hitched."

She had just about persuaded herself to grab her purse and head out to whichever Yonge Street restaurant tickled her fancy when she heard a loud buzz.

Someone calling up from the lobby.

Chapter 13

"It's Cathy. From lunch," the voice said. "Can I come up for a minute?"

Gina hesitated. This was strange! What could she want?

"Sure." She gave directions, and buzzed the door so Cathy could get in.

While waiting, her eyes made a quick sweep of the great room. It was pretty neat. Becki would approve.

With Tony away, there was far less to fuss about. No shoes or briefcase littering the front entry. No ties or jackets hanging over the bar stool. Even the breakfast dishes were nicely stacked in the dishwasher.

She dashed into the washroom to do a last minute check of guest soap and towels.

Three knocks at the door.

Gina pushed down her curiosity and forced a smile on her face. She swung open the door.

Cathy was wearing the same clothes from lunchtime. She held a small brown paper bag. Her smile was rueful.

"I know you said Tony was out of town, so I picked up a couple of sandwiches at Pusateri's. Have you eaten?"

"Cathy, you are a lifesaver!" Gina held the door wide open. "I was just about to get takeout."

Cathy's face beamed. She kicked off her Jimmy Choo heels at the door and walked in, placing the bag on the kitchen island.

"They have the best croissants. I don't allow myself starch at lunch, so a sandwich for dinner is a treat for me. I've got smoked salmon and rare roast beef. We can share if you like."

She sounded shy. Gina had to wonder if she usually ate alone at night. For some reason, she had forgotten to ask if Cathy was married. That is, still married.

"I'll get plates," Gina said.

"I also brought a tiny dessert. We don't have to eat it if you're watching."

Gina smiled to herself.

"A dessert is just what I need tonight. I have a half bottle of Pinot in the fridge."

"That would be lovely," Cathy said. She walked over to the far window. "You have a beautiful view from here. All those lights. It's a really nice condo."

"But too small for the both of us. We're building a house in Caledon. Tony is an architect—but I guess you know that."

Cathy nodded. "My husband was too." She didn't say anymore. Didn't explain if he was retired, dead, or had simply moved on.

Gina busied herself pouring the wine. The silence was a bit awkward. She was trying to figure out how to introduce the subject of why Cathy was here. How did one start a conversation like that? *Thanks for bringing dinner, but why did you do it?*

"You're probably wondering why I'm here," Cathy said. She continued to stare out the window.

Gina started. She picked up both glasses and walked over to the other woman. "Does it have anything to do with our discussion at lunch?"

Cathy took a glass. She brought it to her mouth and took a small sip.

"I wasn't entirely truthful at lunch."

Gina waited.

"Oh, I was telling the truth, but I didn't quite tell everything. Delia...well, she played along."

Gina smiled encouragingly.

Cathy shrugged and turned back to the window.

"I warred with myself all afternoon about whether to come here or not. Delia had phoned and said I should. She said, who could it hurt now? All this happened so long ago. And you really seemed to need this information."

"Hold it right there," Gina said. "I'll just get the sandwiches, so we can eat and chat comfortably. Have a seat on the couch."

Gina dashed back to the kitchen, gathered plates and serviettes, and brought them over to the coffee table. Then she picked up the paper bag with the sandwiches.

"You go ahead and talk while I dish out the goodies."

Cathy smiled then. She seemed less nervous. Then her hands wrapped around her knees, and she frowned.

"That woman. Her name was Linda Davenport. Her husband's name was Garry Davenport."

Gina's hand stopped mid motion. She sucked in air.

"Are you sure?"

She rocked back and forth. "About her name being Linda? I think so. Of course, I can't be absolutely sure it's the woman in the photo. I didn't know her very well. Just to see, really. But I knew him, all right."

The air in the condo got suddenly colder.

"You have to understand. I was a young thing at the time. Impressionable. All this money around. We didn't come from money, so that was new to me. But Bruce—that's my ex—was popular with this crowd. He did a lot of work for them, as an architect."

Gina picked up a half sandwich. She took a small bite and waited.

Cathy stared at the sandwiches. Her hand darted forth and grabbed one. Gina was reminded of a squirrel snatching nuts for winter. It was almost as if Cathy's instinct told her that the good times might be over. The sandwiches might be gone.

"This sounds awful, I know. But I knew Garry well...about as well as you can get. We were having an affair."

The sandwich stopped an inch from Gina's mouth. She hesitated. *What do you say when someone tells you that?*

Then she had it.

"Did Linda know?"

Cathy shook her head. She leaned back on the cushions, clearly relieved. Maybe it was because Gina didn't appear to criticize her.

"She didn't know. No one did, except Delia. That's what made it so exciting." She sounded wistful.

Gina doubted that. Oh, she didn't doubt that it was exciting. But really, could Linda not know that her husband was having an affair? Even though they weren't married yet, Gina was positive she would know if Tony was fooling around.

Wherever Tony was now, she absolutely knew it wasn't with another woman in that way. The funny thing was, she couldn't say why she knew.

Cathy continued to take little bites of the sandwich and swallow them quickly.

"How long had you been seeing each other?" Gina asked. That seemed a nice, non-judgemental way to put it.

"Eight months. It was a miracle it never came up. All through the trial, I was frantic the police or lawyers would show up at the door. But Garry was a prince about it. Never gave me away."

She sighed.

"You can't imagine what a magical time it was for me, those eight months. I was feeling as guilty as hell, of course. Bruce was a good guy. But he wasn't...exciting. Garry was older and so sophisticated. He knew how to talk to a girl to make her feel special. I know it sounds creepy, but believe me, he wasn't."

That was exactly how it sounded to Gina! A suave, older man taking advantage of a younger star-struck woman. It was a pattern as old as time.

Even now, having never met the great Garry Davenport, Gina felt animosity toward him.

"Tell me about the last time you saw him."

Cathy's blue-grey eyes darted to the plate. She reached for another sandwich. Her hand paused over the smoked salmon, wavering there. Instead, she snatched the roast beef.

"I'd seen Garry on the Monday night. Then Tuesday, he didn't phone. I found out through the papers that he'd been arrested. I was just about frantic."

She played with the half sandwich in her hand. One manicured finger stroked the open end absently.

"You can't imagine what a nightmare it was for me. I never saw him again. He never tried to contact me. Made sure that there were no links the investigators could follow. It broke my heart, but I knew why he was doing it. He'd warned me it could happen."

Gina cleared her throat. "Why was that, do you think? Was he protecting you from the press?"

Cathy put down the sandwich and reached for her wine glass.

"Not only them. He had some pretty powerful mob contacts. People he wouldn't talk about. I think he was scared of them."

It was after ten when Cathy left. Gina sat back to contemplate this new information. She thought about phoning Becki, but she knew Karl went to bed early because of the job. This could wait until morning.

So Louisa could be Linda Davenport. Delia seemed to think she was. Cathy couldn't be positive of course.

Gina tried to add up the evidence, however meagre.

If Louisa was Linda, she'd kept the same initials for her new name. What had been her maiden name? Had she reverted to that as well? That would be initial proof. They would have to research that.

Then there was the evidence of the dress. Delia had described the very gown Gina had seen hanging in Louisa's closet.

Tony would dismiss that of course. Most men would. It was so long ago, after all. But women remembered things like that. And Gina knew that it was very unlikely there would be two women with the same Clotheslines dress. Too much of a coincidence, when you were talking couture. These things weren't sold by the dozen.

Louisa had kept that dress. She had, in fact, treasured it. Gina knew that from experience. You didn't keep old evening gowns for years and years unless you were really attached to them, or extremely sentimental. They simply took up too much room.

She was deep in thought when the phone rang.

Chapter 14

The confusion of silhouettes was the result of too many light sources—the moon that hung bright in the sky, streetlights, more plentiful than usual car headlights, emergency vehicle strobes and the glow from the fire which domed the southwest quadrant of town.

Becki quickened her pace.

She could see the tops of the flames above the roofs of all the other structures. That's how big the fire was. That's how she knew there would be nothing salvageable after the blaze was extinguished.

She rounded the last corner and the burning house came into full view. She came to a stop, then slowly she forced herself forward to join the circle of onlookers at the perimeter of the scene. For a long while she just bore witness along with the rest of them. Lost in her thoughts.

Karl is here somewhere among all the professionals and volunteers working hard to bring the situation under control.

Then bits of conversation began to register.

"I wonder how it started."

"The house must have been empty."

"Vandals, do you think?"

"Kids fooling around?

"A freak accident?"

"Could it have been deliberate?"

"It was such a beautiful old house."

"Poor Louisa. It's the final insult, isn't it?"

Becki opened her mouth and found herself asking the group immediately to her right, "Did you know Louisa well?"

The only one to reply was a young girl in her early twenties. A woman really, but to Becki she was still a girl. Her sandy beach-coloured hair was gathered in a ponytail and fell to her waist. Her flawless skin made her just right for a Calvin Klein ad for perfume.

"I knew her pretty well," the girl said. "I cleaned her house." She shook her head with regret. The light from the fire was warm-toned and flattering.

Becki asked, "How long did you work there?" The girl was one of those creatures whose natural magnetism draws all those around.

"About three years," she said.

"Once a week for three years," Becki calculated out loud.

"Yup."

"Such a shock that Louisa's gone, isn't it?" Becki introduced herself then, and added, "I run the décor shop Beautiful Things."

The girl nodded, and yet it didn't look like she quite pinpointed Becki's place in Black Currant Bay society.

"On Main Street," Becki supplied. "We renovated Louisa's kitchen. She was my client." It would be pushing it to include the words "and my friend" so she didn't.

"Pleased to meet you, Becki. I'm Sylvia." Sylvia smiled. Her charm brightened the sombre night.

Just then someone grabbed Becki's arm, startling her at first, but it was Lottie.

"I can't take any more of this," Lottie whispered low and urgently.

Remembering how at Gina's shower Lottie was understandably still very distraught about losing her best friend, Becki sympathised. "This is especially hard on you."

"I can't bear it!" Lottie cried. Suddenly she whirled on her heels and pointed at the inferno. "See the ghosts?" There was a fierceness to her stance.

Watching Lottie gesticulating at the fire tugged at Becki's heartstrings.

If ever there were a night for ghosts in Black Currant Bay, she thought, *this is it.* However, she chose to gently assure the elderly woman beside her, "No, I don't see any ghosts."

Luckily Lottie didn't put up an argument. She loosened her posture and turned her back to the fire. Changing the subject she asked, "Is Gina here with you, Becki?" She darted her eyes among the throngs of people.

"Gina's back home in Toronto."

Lottie slumped further. Then her eyes brightened. "Do you know Gina?" she asked Sylvia, addressing the girl for the first time. "Gina Monroe."

"Isn't she the reporter on The Weather Network?"

"That's her. Do you know that she's Becki's honorary niece? We had a wedding shower for her last week. What a lovely woman! More beautiful in person than she is on the screen. Absolutely Stunning!" Lottie gazed shyly up at Sylvia. "You're quite beautiful yourself."

"Thank you." Sylvia shrugged.

"Wish I had a daughter," Lottie continued. "A lovely girl to warm a mother's heart."

Becki remembered how lonely Lottie seemed. Lots of talk of a trip back home to Cornwall but no one to go with now that Louisa was gone. And no one to stay with once she was over there apparently.

Becki tried to draw both women into conversation. "How did you learn of the fire?" she asked.

Sylvia pointed to herself. "I was driving home from Casinoarama. It was on the news on my car radio."

"Were you coming home from a show?" Becki asked. Every now and then she and Karl caught a performance by an old favourite on stage there.

"Not this time. I was just playin' the slots."

Lottie asked, "What's a young thing like you doing cooping herself up with those blasted buzzing machines?"

Becki was glad it was Lottie who put that question out there because there was a judgmental ring to it. However, she wondered the exact same thing herself.

"Well to answer your question, one of these days I'm going to hit the jackpot of all jackpots and I'll be out of here," Sylvia lifted both arms in pre-celebration, "in the blink of an eye!"

"The odds are always in favour of the house." Lottie sounded knowledgeable.

"So they say. But I'm a Players Club member. If I don't win cash every time, I win points," Sylvia said.

"And how are points going to help you?"

Becki was staying out of this.

"I can use them to see concerts and in all the casino restaurants."

"Exactly. They aren't stupid down there at Casinoarama. They give you points so you'll come back and spend more money in their establishment. It's only real money that you can spend anywhere you like."

Becki figured Sylvia was holding back from verbally lashing out at Lottie's admonishments. The reason for her restraint, she assumed, was the sombre nature of the event that had drawn them together, literally standing in the light of the destruction of the last piece of evidence that a woman had lived in their community.

In a few moments Becki wandered away on her own. She checked out her fellow citizens gathered where town met lake. She recognized the majority of them. And she was sure they recognized her. Maybe they didn't really know each other but the town was small so they ran into each other at the pharmacy, at the grocery store, at the post office... There weren't very many strangers in Black Currant Bay. She herself was one of the last newcomers to settle in.

That would all change if that guy who was proposing a new development on the waterfront—what was his name? Spellman?—had his way. Was he perhaps watching the evening unwind with a smirk on his face?

"Oh, there's Kathleen!" Becki exclaimed on a happy breath. She ran over to her friend. "You're here too!"

"Yeah, couldn't sleep. Can you believe I can hear the commotion from my house, which as you know is five streets over? Plus the eerie orange glow I see every time I look out my bedroom window is disconcerting."

"It's going to be a long night."

"What do you think happened?" Kathleen asked.

There was a glint in her eyes which Becki attributed to nervous excitement. Kathleen was always at the centre of things. She cut a flamboyant figure, always full of enthusiasm and zest for life. She lived large and single after her divorce from Henry. Kathleen was a successful romance novelist.

"It's not hard coming up with theories," Becki admitted.

"Hit me."

"There's the one about the developer who burns down this unused house because he thinks it will facilitate his building project. There's the local group of teenagers that sneaks inside the empty house to do drugs and leaves behind a butt smouldering on a rug." Becki looked up at Kathleen and winked. "Not to mention the possibility it's Louisa's murderer who came back to the scene of the crime to eliminate some clue he left behind."

"You never did lack for imagination."

"Unfortunately that's not what counts in crime investigation. Karl keeps reminding me of that."

"Party pooper."

"Well, it's one thing to think creatively and come up with a whole realm of possibilities. It's quite another thing to be able pick out which one of them is real. And prove it."

"Can I walk you home?" Becki continued. "Think you're ready?"

"That would take you the long, long way around," Kathleen said.

"But I want your company."

She wasn't sure Kathleen had the right sort of personality to provide soothing comfort but she was one of two great friends Becki had in Black Currant Bay. And since she knew Karl wouldn't be able to come home until the wee hours of morning, if then...

Kathleen must have understood Becki's need because they walked a block up the hill in total silence, trailed by the lake breeze carrying the stench of fire.

Chapter 15

Lottie continued to gaze at the smoldering wreckage of Louisa's former home.

So many pleasant hours had been spent there, drinking coffee with delicious treats in the beautiful living room. Sipping iced tea in the back garden, with the sounds of birds and insects to keep them company.

Alone or with others, gossiping or merely enjoying each other's company, this routine had been a treasured part of Lottie's life for over twenty years.

And now Louisa was gone. Even her house was gone.

It was the smell that made her weak. The incredible acrid odour of burned things. It hung in the evening sky, cloaking the entire town.

Fire, they say, is cleansing, but there is nothing pure about the residue, Lottie thought.

Charred wood floors and beams, burned upholstery and clothing—it was all a mess. Now everything was completely soaked with water from the hoses. Even the beautiful flowerbeds had turned to churned mud. Everything was wrecked. It made one sick to contemplate the contents of a whole lifetime on earth being destroyed in mere minutes.

Still, she watched and waited.

She needed to be there. As Louisa was her friend, it was her duty to be there until the end. In fact, it was the least she could do, under the circumstances. But everything in her had to fight the fear that threatened to overwhelm her and leave her babbling.

These regular people like Becki and Sylvia couldn't see beyond this world—they had no idea what real fear was. Lottie almost pitied them in a way.

What they couldn't see is that this world didn't *matter*. It was only passing. And yes, you could hurt and become ill in this world—go hungry and be cold—but that was a short passage compared to *what awaited on the other side*.

The ghosts were gone now. They had left the burning house. Firemen still climbed all over the wreckage, but Lottie ignored them.

Soon she would take her trip to Cornwall. There, she would find answers to the questions that had haunted her since childhood.

It was most important that she go to Cornwall.

"Move back, ma'am." A nice young policeman was waving his arm at her. He was fair-haired and broad-shouldered, like she imagined Becki's husband Karl might have looked thirty years ago.

Lottie gazed up at him, way up. She smiled like a girl, and one hand played absently with a stray lock of grey hair. Tall men made her feel giddy.

He moved on. She turned away and started toward home.

How smart, that she had not waited to retrieve those things from Louisa's home. Things that should have been hers anyway, as Louisa was gone now. It was only right.

Something had compelled her, warned her to act fast. Moving around that house that night with the ghosts still there had been the hardest thing she had ever done.

A chill came over her. Maybe not. Maybe the second hardest. *Why is nothing ever as you think it will be?*

As she walked further away, the air became fresher. It was possible to breathe normally again. The nightmare receded.

Lottie had just passed Pine Street when another horrible thought came to her. Would this fire make a difference to her inheritance? She gasped. What if the house wasn't insured? Did insurance lapse automatically if you died?

What if there wasn't enough money to go to Cornwall?

It was wonderful to have a day off work. As Gina sipped coffee in her mother's meticulously kept uptown house, she marvelled how you can have the best job in the world, and still want a break from it.

Anna had called last night, suggesting Gina stop by. It was wonderful, having her mom in the same city. Yes, her parents traveled more now that her dad had retired, but still, this long low city bungalow from the 1970s was a retreat she just loved.

Tony had helped her parents restore it with care. An earlier renovation had removed some of the original charm of the era. Tony had done a careful job respecting the past and correcting what he could to bring the home back to the architect's vision. The pecan wood floor was original, as was the white angel stone fireplace. The original floor to ceiling windows had been replaced, but the view to the ravine out the back was stunning in all seasons.

"Good thing Cathy didn't swear you to secrecy," her mother said.

Gina looked up. "I would have told you anyway, Mom." She didn't keep things like this from her mother.

Anna's smile was a beautiful thing. "But I'm wondering if she didn't try to make you promise on purpose. Maybe she needed to confess for her soul."

Gina considered that. "You might be right. I could almost see relief cross her face, the second she finished telling me."

"Imagine keeping something secret like that for so long. I imagine it must have been lonely."

Gina started. "Lonely?" Such a strange word for her mom to use.

Anna shrugged. "She had the romance of her lifetime. One of those one in a million things, at least from her point of view. But she couldn't tell anyone about it. Not even when it was over, because of fear."

"Except Delia. Delia knew."

Anna raised an eyebrow. "Really? She didn't let on, at lunch."

"Delia prompted her to tell me. I'm not sure Cathy would have otherwise."

"You could be right. She would have been afraid back then. I imagine that fear doesn't completely go away with time."

Gina digested that. Fear of legal entanglements, she could imagine. Her lover had been convicted, after all. The police might have considered Cathy a possible accessory to his financial crimes, and at least questioned her. Then there was the possibility of mob connections.

Yes, it made sense. Cathy had been wise to stay as mum as possible through the years.

"A romance of a lifetime with a notorious modern day robber-baron. It does have an operatic quality to it."

"Have you told Becki yet?"

Gina shook her head. "Wanted to bounce it off you first. Thing is, I like Cathy."

"So do I."

They were silent a minute.

"So you understand what I'm thinking."

"That telling Becki will mean she has to tell Karl? And then the police will probably contact her? I think it's okay, Gina. She wouldn't have come over last night to talk to you if she wasn't prepared to face the music now."

Would there be much music to be faced?

"But surely, since her ex-lover was already convicted, the police won't need to question her. The trial was over years ago. I bet all the people involved are retired, even."

Anna looked up sharply. "I wasn't thinking of that, Gina. I was thinking how it might have a bearing on what happened re that poor woman's death."

Gina looked down at her coffee cup. Villeroy & Boch, she noted. A vivid winter scene from a famous museum painting had been meticulously reproduced onto it. Even for every day, her mother took pleasure in using beautiful things.

"Mom, you can't honestly think Cathy had anything to do with that."

Anna rose gracefully from the family room couch. She walked over to the kitchen counter and poured more coffee from the carafe into the china mug. She added a small amount of cream from the porcelain pitcher. No sugar.

"Of course I don't. But not because I think Cathy is incapable of it. Most of us are capable of killing strangers if we or our loved ones are threatened. Heck, many people will even kill people they care about."

"That's a sobering thought," Gina said. But they both knew it to be true. They both carried the scars from that horrible time. The trial was still going on.

Anna leaned over the ochre granite counter and rested her elbows on it.

"But no, I don't think Cathy had anything to do with Becki's friend's death. More because I can't think of a single reason why she would gain from it."

Either could Gina. Why kill the estranged wife of the man you had an affair with over twenty years ago? How could that possibly matter now? Especially if the ex-wife didn't know you had been his mistress.

Besides, Cathy was divorced now. She appeared to be well off. Better off than Louisa, in any case.

Still, it was an angle. They needed to explore all leads.

"Even so, I should tell Becki," Gina said.

"Of course you should, darling. It doesn't pay to keep secrets. Never does. Except if someone asks you how they look, of course."

"'Does this make me look fat?'" Gina grinned. She looked over at her mother, so neatly dressed in Ralph Lauren, from head to toe. "No chance there. You look terrific for fifty."

"Gina, I'm nearly sixty."

"Just as I said."

Anna laughed.

But Gina was swept back to thoughts of secrets. *It doesn't pay to keep secrets*, her mother had said. *But what if you had to? What if your job demanded it?*

"Have you heard from Tony?"

Her head shot up. Why is it mothers almost always knew exactly what you were thinking?

They were both startled by the cellphone ringing.

"Take it," Anna said. "I'll just use the loo."

When she got back a few minutes later, Gina was still on the phone, pacing the floor. Her eyes were wide.

"Well, that lets Cathy out. She was at my place last night from eight until ten. Just a sec," she said into the phone. "I have to tell Mom."

"You won't believe this." She covered the phone's speaker with her hand. "It's Becki. Louisa's house burned down last night. It was completely destroyed along with everything in it."

Anna gasped. "Was anyone hurt?"

Gina shook her head. "But Karl thinks it was arson."

Chapter 16

There was a small memorial for Louisa on Sunday.

Everyone who was at the shower attended the memorial. Of course Gina could be excused because she was just a visitor to Black Currant Bay and also because her wedding day was less than two weeks away.

Becki and Karl attended together. In addition to the shower ladies, there was Louisa's cleaning lady, the two cops who had worked with Karl at the scene of the crime, the ambulance crew. The local pharmacist was there. The local doctor. The small church was crowded with people despite the fact that no one had yet "claimed" Louisa. This was what small towns were like. Even if you didn't know the deceased well, you came out of respect.

There's a popular theory which suggests that clues to a crime can be gathered at a funeral or memorial, signs of guilt detected among the mourners. Karl was in fact keeping his eyes open to all possibilities. So were his officers. But Becki didn't think much would be uncovered here.

Everyone was on their best behaviour. Everyone knew they were being watched. If not for signs of guilt, for signs of emotion.

If it were true that evidence of extreme emotion signalled guilt, Becki was in big trouble herself. She had felt tears of outrage threaten at the entrance to the red brick chapel. The first hymn brought those tears to the brink of her lower eyelids and by the time the reverend was saying a few words about gentle townswoman Louisa they were rolling down her face.

Douglas Spellman walked into Beautiful Things on Monday hopefully for the last time in his life, his discerning blue eyes seeking out Rebekkah Green, co-proprietor. She ought to be right up front waiting for him because he'd met her half-sister and business partner two Saturdays ago and had set up a meeting for today. He was actually a few power minutes late.

Although his entry through the front door triggered what sounded like a sleigh bell—thankfully not an unpleasant sound—he was kept waiting in the entrance. He adjusted his tie. Still no one appeared. Apparently he would have to make his way through the store to wherever Rebekkah kept an office. Surely she didn't expect him to go to the counter where he'd first spoken to her sister Anne. After all he wasn't just a regular customer.

He marched up the closest aisle, which also seemed like the most direct route to the back, and as he passed by the spools of fabric lining the wall he brushed them with his fingertips. This served to confirm that the fabrics displayed were of good quality and that there was a decent selection of weights and textures. Meanwhile, his eyes observed once again that Ms. Rebekkah Green of Beautiful Things was discriminating with colour and pattern.

Yes, he'd invited two Toronto design firms to quote on the Black Currant Bay project and he could have left it at that, assured of professionalism and style, but something told him that getting on the good side of some of the citizens of this town would be an excellent way to grease the wheels.

Of course there are other ways.

The large quantity of textiles muffled the store's acoustics but now he could hear two women in conversation. He rounded a corner and saw them leaning over a pile of area rugs.

One of the women was easily forgettable as far as he was concerned. He supposed she must be a local housewife looking for some help with her home.

However the other woman impressed. She stood above average in height for a woman, maybe five feet six, he thought. She had long, lustrous dark hair, pale white skin. Her inherently elegant movements reminded him of the lovely Nigella Lawson or maybe even Catherine Zeta-Jones, but she was closer in age to Nigella.

She wore reasonable pumps, black leggings, and she nicely filled out a fitted paisley tunic with three quarter sleeves. Classic lines with very little adornment. *She understands the understated.*

With a smile on his face he approached. "Hello, Ms. Green. I'm Douglas Spellman. We have an appointment?" He allowed his last sentence to end with just the slightest of upturns. Barely enough to make it a question. Then he extended his hand in her direction.

"Oh hello, Mr. Spellman." She shook his hand. "I'll be right with you. Marion has just about made her final decision about this rug for her bedroom." She lifted a corner for him to see. "What do you think?"

Well, he could care less what Marion bought for her bedroom but Rebekkah put him on the spot. He turned to the client and said, "I'm sure whatever Ms. Green and you choose will be perfect." *There.*

"Call me Becki. Everyone does. Have a seat in our little design nook over there and I'll be right with you." She pointed and grinned pleasantly.

Bitch!

Once Becki had rung up Marion's invoice, arranged for delivery, and chatted with her all the way to the door where she said a warm good-bye, she headed to the corner nook she and Anne had set up so customers could browse through wallpaper books in comfort.

"I'm sorry about the delay," she said. "Thank you for being so patient—may I call you Douglas?" Before he could reply she continued. "It's only either Anne or myself in the store at one time. Black Currant Bay is just too small for us to be able to afford to double up. Now tell me a little more about your project so I can get a feel for what sort of ambiance you're looking for."

She sat down on the couch opposite him and crossed her legs. She leaned forward with interest after grabbing her notebook and pencil from the side table.

He swivelled his laptop computer on the coffee table between them so she could see the screen on which a slideshow was playing.

The photography was beautiful. Gulls floating in blue skies, aerials of the lake and the beach and the little town snuggled in the forest, a shot of the quaint downtown.

The mock-ups and elevations that Douglas presented of the homes themselves were intriguing as well. Becki was relieved to see that the architect had not transposed Venice, Italy, to Black Currant Bay, Canada. Opulent yes. But the development was conceived in a style that complemented its proposed location.

"We're appealing to owners with multi-million-dollar lifestyles," Douglas specified. Then he paused.

If he's expecting my jaw to drop he's sadly mistaken.

Unbeknownst to most of the citizens of Black Currant Bay, Becki came from money. Therefore she was not awestruck by affluence. Equally she wasn't reverse prejudiced against the wealthy. But, man, she couldn't stand arrogance!

When Douglas didn't get the reaction he hoped for, he repeated the slogan that Anne had advised her of.

"Small-town Black Currant Bay—Port to the World."

Becki noticed he fingered the knot of his tie as if it were a talisman of worldliness.

"Very nice," she said. "Yes, so…nautical, blue, white, turquoise. Do you propose that these will be summer homes only?"

She found herself fighting a dislike for this man. It was true that she played with the idea that he was behind the destruction of Louisa's home, if not the destruction of Louisa herself. But innocent until proven guilty.

"Oh yes. Summer only. Our buyers will spend winters in the southern States and the Caribbean. I'm talking very select occupants."

"But you probably want a cottagey feel to the interiors. These are vacation homes, after all. Nothing too formal or stiff. Something relaxed and soothing."

"Yes, I suppose."

He can see reason.

Becki jotted down notes. "What do you think of a bit of whimsy for the sales centre and model home? Something to remind buyers of the fun they would have if they moved here? Maybe even a touch of retro? Retro is hot right now."

"Not antiques!"

"No, not for this. I'm thinking 70s accessories."

He nodded his head as he did many times over the course of their discussion. It seemed she and her work fared well in his esteem. After a while, she had verbal approval of the plan she had in mind. She would formalize it later in her written presentation.

Now it came time to dig into something else. She closed her notebook.

"You know," she said, "you look familiar to me, Douglas." She wasn't above using that old pick-up line. She knew he would feel flattered if she showed personal interest. Most men were.

"I know this is the first time we've met formally, but I feel like I've seen you around town. Where was it I wonder?" She made like she was thinking back. Of course she really was.

Just her imagination or did a sudden wariness come into his eyes?

"I don't know where you would have seen me. I was here in your store last Saturday as you know. Been scouting around here a few times before that but most of my work is done from my office in Toronto."

"Was it at Louisa's memorial?" She purposefully lit up her eyes with near recognition. "Or was it at Louisa's house before she died? Did you know Louisa Davidson?"

He squirmed.

"Now I've got it, I saw you at Louisa's not last Friday but the one before! I was on a boat with my friend Gina Monroe from The Weather Network"—*a reliable witness*—"and we saw you from the water."

"Um..." He was obviously too uncomfortable to question how they could possibly have recognized him from so far away. Or maybe he pictured them close to shore in a canoe.

Becki didn't bring up binoculars.

"What would you have been doing there? Because, um, wasn't that the day after Louisa died?" She let her words trail off.

Obviously she wasn't worried about whether or not she got the Spellman account.

But he seemed anxious to clear up any misunderstanding.

"Since I'm planning this development up here, I keep up with the *Black Currant Bay Beacon Star* online."

"Yes, I'm sure you would."

"I happened on Louisa's obituary and the call for next of kin. Her address was included."

"Mmm-hmm?"

"Wanted to see if her property would fit my resort."

By that time he had regained his composure and seemed oblivious to how much he came off like an ambulance chaser.

Becki wondered, *Is he telling the whole truth?* Then she worried, *Have I let my anger about Louisa's death push me too far? I basically served Gina and myself up to this stranger as two eyewitnesses.*

Witnesses?

To what exactly?

A survey of the land of a dead woman? Or a return to the scene of a crime?

In a gesture that was as unconscious as it was revealing, she crossed her arms in front of her body.

This is not like me.

I let myself get carried away. And after instructing Gina that we need to be careful.

Chapter 17

Gina walked off the set and threw herself into an empty desk chair. She kicked off her Italian heels, and sighed with relief. Dave on Camera One gave her a thumbs up sign. She smiled in return.

It was late afternoon, and time for Chris to take over the broadcast. *Thank goodness.*

Gina loved her job on The Weather Network, but it was always a relief to sit down. The trouble with being on TV is you were standing all the time. Already this year she had reduced her shoe heel height from over three inches, to two and a half. At this rate, soon she would be wearing flats.

Gina sighed again. This was definitely a young person's job. And she knew better than to complain out loud. She'd been damned lucky to land this job right after school. Yes, the degree in meteorology had been essential. But others had that. And yes, she had style, and apparently a good face for the camera. But there would be hundreds of young, good-looking hopefuls waiting in the wings for this job when she left. Gina was entirely realistic about that.

Brenda, one of the producers, brought over a bottle of water for her.

"Thanks," Gina said gratefully. She smiled up at the smartly-dressed middle-aged woman.

Brenda didn't look happy. In fact, there were deep furls in her usually smooth forehead. "You may need something stronger after you see this." She held out the Toronto morning paper. The national one, with the big circulation.

Gina took it with one hand. She unfolded it.

"Check the bottom," Brenda said.

Gina's eyes travelled down.

Weather Network Star Discovers Murder Victim

Gina Monroe of The Weather Network is a key witness in the murder of a local woman in the small northern town of Black Currant Bay. Sources say Ms. Monroe discovered the body in the victim's home, which was to be the site of Ms. Monroe's wedding shower the next day.
The victim is said to be Louisa Davidson, a long-time resident of Black Currant Bay. The cause of death has not been confirmed. Police are treating this as a homicide.
Also at the scene was Rebekkah Green, wife of the Black Currant Bay Chief of Police, and friend of Ms. Monroe.
Gina Monroe (29) is a well-known celebrity in the Toronto area, and a familiar face on the charity gala circuit. She is engaged to marry Anthony Ferrero (34), the award-winning architect...

Gina's hand started to shake. She nearly dropped the paper. What would Becki say when she saw this? Karl was going to have a fit. And Tony! They even mentioned Tony. He was going to go ballistic.

"Oh my God," said Gina out loud. "How the hell did they get this information?"

"So it's true?" Brenda asked. "Shit, Gina. Why didn't you tell me?"

Gina looked up. She felt her mouth go dry. She looked down at the paper. They had even used a stock photo of her and Tony at a charity gala. There she was, smiling directly at the camera, in that sapphire blue Galliano that had cost the earth...

Back to earth. Why hadn't she told anyone?

"It never occurred to me. I didn't think it would get out. Nobody down here cares about a small town death way up north." Even as she uttered the words, she knew they sounded callous.

"They may not care about *her*, but the media cares about *you*. You are news down here. People will buy this paper just to read that story." Brenda sat down in a chair opposite.

"I just never dreamed the story would get down here. I'm so sorry."

Gina glanced down at the paper again, to read the rest of the article. But it just seemed to be words on a page. She couldn't concentrate. Brenda wouldn't stop talking.

"Ted called me right away. I've got our PR people waiting in the meeting room. I didn't want to take you off the air, so they've been waiting. Gina, you've got to tell them everything. We have to manage this carefully."

Now her head shot up. Brenda was staring at her. Gina felt a chill go down her back.

There was a moment of silence.

"Don't panic," said Brenda. She reached forward to pat Gina's knee. "We've got the best."

The best what, thought Gina? *The best PR people to protect the station?*

"One good thing though." The producer rose to her feet. "Nothing like a little press to help the numbers. Your viewership today has been through the roof."

Gina drove home in a fog. She waited until getting into the condo elevator before checking her cellphone.

Six calls from her mother. Two from Becki. More from various friends and relatives. One from the wedding planner.

Four calls from media personalities.

She focussed on the Becki calls. Both times, Becki had said, "Call me when you get this."

Obviously, Becki knew. Gina closed her eyes. Her wedding was little more than a week away, and the next few days were going to be an ordeal.

The elevator doors opened. She moved swiftly to the condo door and used her key to open it.

Gina stepped inside. For a split second, she tensed, sensing the presence of someone else in the room.

She swung around to the kitchen.

Tony stood there, with both arms crossed.

"What the hell is going on, Gina?"

Twenty minutes later, the urgent phone calls had been made. Mothers had been placated. Aunts had been reassured.

They sat on the sofa in the condo, waiting. Both waiting for the other to bring it up.

Gina turned her attention to Tony.

"So where were you?"

Tony held the mug of coffee in both hands. How the heck he could drink caffeine at night and still fall right to sleep was a mystery to her.

Yet another mystery.

"Montreal. Like I said."

Gina stared at him. He looked tired. The rigid look to his body had passed and been replaced by weariness. His brown hair was dishevelled, and his blue eyes drooped.

Did she believe him? No question, he must have been close by, to get back to Toronto in less than eight hours.

"Did the newspaper article bring you back?"

He sipped from the mug. "I was coming anyway. I saw the paper on the plane."

The plane from where, she thought. But it would do no good to ask again, she knew.

"But it would have," Tony said. "Brought me back."

Gina felt his eyes on her now.

"Whatever you think, I love you, Gina. The thought of you being in danger drives me berserk." He paused. His hands fiddled with the mug. "I have a few things to clean up. That's all."

She stared down at the hands in her lap.

"The wedding is just over a week away," she said simply.

"I know when the wedding is," Tony said.

"So it's out of the bag," Becki said, after hanging up the phone.

Karl threw himself down in an easy chair. "I'm sorry. I don't know how Toronto media got hold of the details."

"Did someone in the department leak it?"

Karl shrugged. His large body moved forward so that his elbows rested on his knees. His hands went to hold his head. Fingers raked through the thick hair.

"It shouldn't have happened. That local reporter might have a friend on the force. Hard to keep something like this quiet with Gina involved."

Becki hesitated. She should tell Karl about the meeting with the developer today. That it had been the developer who had cased Louisa's property. But something more important was haunting her.

"Does this put Gina in any danger, do you think?"

Karl shook his head. "Can't see how. So she discovered the body. Why would that make a difference?"

"But..." *Well, darn,* thought Becki. *Maybe I'm being too paranoid. The newspaper article just said that Gina had been at the scene of the crime. It didn't say anything about her searching the house with me after, or doing any sleuthing.*

"Did they say anything about the fire?"

"What?" said Becki, lost in thought.

"The fire. Did the newspaper mention the fire that burned down the vic's house? It might be important."

Becki moved her head to meet his eyes. "Gina didn't say. And I forgot to ask."

She knew what Karl was going to say next. He was going to suggest they stop investigating Louisa's past.

But Karl knew her better than that. The poor woman had been murdered. Becki felt it was their duty to do everything possible to help solve the mystery of who Louisa really was. Gina's connections in Toronto were just too good to pass up.

"Before you say it…"

Karl grunted. "You know exactly what I'm going to say, don't you."

Becki smiled. "Most of the time."

Chapter 18

After all these years, he had finally found Linda. Not that it had worked out the way he had planned.

Linda was dead now.

Bad thing, good thing as people often said these days, and it was as good a way as any to explain how it hurt like hell—because he loved her once—and yet it pleased him too, because she was no longer out there somewhere, holding onto that crucial piece of evidence that could send him right back to the slammer.

Which left only one question. *Did her secret die with her?*

That question was paramount, and why he couldn't allow himself to wallow in self-pity about how he'd messed his life up so badly. Also why he was all the way out here in Oakville, and sending every contact he could still count on out scrounging here, there and everywhere for information.

Garry Davenport's spine tingled. That familiar sign of fear and adrenaline. He pushed back against the leather upholstery of his Audi.

He exited off the 403 onto Dundas Street West and drove north. Almost immediately he turned right onto Hyde Park Gate, and then right again onto Bristol Circle. His vehicle floated quietly along the road.

It was cool enough this evening to buzz down the windows and get some air but he preferred to keep the tinted glass up. You never knew if there were cameras.

Paranoia.

Okay, so a camera wouldn't easily catch who was driving, but it would still catch his licence plate number. Hold on a minute. He was getting way ahead of himself. The cops may never have to go looking for camera footage. They may not have to get involved at all. It depended...

There it is!

On his right-hand side as he rounded the curve. Exactly as expected. He'd done his homework. Nowadays it was all too easy, because everything and anything was displayed for all to see on the Internet.

A custom-built facility, clearly marked number 2655, no sidewalk along the curbed road—industrial parks are never pedestrian friendly—gated entrances, typical landscaping, including irrigated lawns, beds of tall grasses and neon marigolds, a few small trees. The parking lots in the front and the back of the building were flooded with white light from commercial lampposts. The building itself looked generous in size with glass and stucco panels forming basic rectangles.

This was the home of The Weather Network.

Gina tried to explain to Tony how she was feeling.

"You tell me I should mind my own business and not get involved and stay safe, and here you are cavorting around the world on secret agent missions. Talk about a double standard."

"Gina, I'm a trained professional."

"And you're doing trained professional stuff. I'm just following up on a few dresses, trying to find someone's next of kin. Where's the harm in that? Besides, I have a knack for investigation whether you want to admit it or not. I'm a freaking reporter after all!"

"A weather reporter."

"There you go being condescending again." She turned her head. She didn't even want to look at him now.

"Okay, what if I admit you do have a talent for investigation? What if it's exactly that that scares me?"

"Maybe we're finally getting somewhere," Gina said.

"I don't think you're going to be any happier with what logically comes next, Gina."

"Try me." She crossed her arms.

"Your interest in—and talent for—looking into things like this murder in Black Currant Bay scares me because you probably do know enough to get yourself in trouble but you don't have the skills or the backup or the...weapons to defend yourself if you turn over something unexpected and the shit really hits the fan."

Gina glared at him.

"So to speak."

"Like what's going to happen?"

"Exactly. Unknown factor."

"Let me see if I've got this straight. You don't want me to get involved in something that has an unknown factor," she drew air quotes around those two words, "because of fear for my safety."

"Yes." Tony sounded relieved.

But Gina hadn't finished. "Yet I'm supposed to be okay with you flying off to who knows where doing who knows what and not be concerned about *your* safety."

"We're just going in circles."

A very analytical, male thing to say as far as she was concerned. Even if it were true they were going round and round on the same topic, every time they rehashed the material, a little more nuance was added to the conversation.

"Tell me how my looking into a bunch of clothes and finding out someone's secret past can lead to mortal danger," she challenged. She'd explained to Tony everything she'd discovered so far and instead of praise, she'd gotten nothing but grief.

"First of all, Louisa, or Linda if you're on the right track, was obviously in jeopardy for some reason and here you are immersing yourself in her world. If you don't know the cause of the threat to her safety, how can you avoid it yourself?"

Maybe he has a point. "I'm keeping an arm's distance away." That sounded lame even to her. Funny, despite Becki's warnings, Gina had never felt any trepidation whatsoever. Until now. Tony's fierce defence of his point of view was starting to scare her a teeny bit. Weaken her resolve just a tad. Her upper lip trembled.

He must have sensed the change in Gina. He put his arm around her and squeezed. "You're thinking too linearly, my love," he said, his voice more tender than it had been all night. "In your mind, one fact leads to the next which then leads to a third fact in a natural sequence."

"The line is not always straight," argued Gina.

"I'll give you that. But have you considered lateral connections? Danger often flies in tangentially."

"Oh." She thought on that.

Tony seemed content to hold her in his arms.

It came to her. Something she of all people should never have overlooked. Little did he know it but by explaining his way of thinking, Tony had handed Gina a new angle on the case. And this time she wasn't going to breathe a word of it to him.

All he'd done since he got back was admonish her for her risky behaviour and he hadn't explained the truth about where he had been or what he had been doing and it didn't sound like he was anywhere near ready to either.

It felt like they were growing further apart instead of closer together. As she'd reminded Tony, their wedding was just over a week away.

Should I postpone it?

Sad to say but there was no easy answer. Stopping everything at this late date seemed too drastic to contemplate. But continuing on as if everything was hunky dory seemed just as radically wrong. She'd have to wait until one option clearly outweighed the other.

When Gina's heart sank like this, it felt like her whole being sank right along with it. The tender skin under her eyes, the apples of her cheeks, the corners of her mouth, the set of her chin, the frame of her shoulders... They all hollowed and drooped and fell and dipped and slumped.

The only thing that made her feel better was her plan to call Becki and tell her what she'd just figured out, thanks in part to Tony.

Since he probably wasn't going anywhere tonight, the call would have to wait until tomorrow. In the meantime she would just have to pretend that everything was fine. Didn't happiness gurus say you should act it until you feel it?

Chapter 19

Okay, so he'd been stupid. Stupid to go to her workplace, without even checking to see when she would be there. These television personalities didn't keep regular hours. He should have remembered that. After all, the entertainment world had been his business for decades. All those years in prison had obviously done something to soften to his brain.

Garry Davenport was back in the Audi, staring out the windshield without seeing. His mind was a muddle.

It would have been so damned easy. Just check on The Weather Network itself. Watch for the shift she worked, then arrange to be there in the parking lot when she got off.

Follow her home.

He cursed at his own stupidity. Impatience—that had always been his weakness. Now he had wasted a day. Not only that, he had exposed himself to the girl at reception.

Her sunny smile had turned to a frown when she heard the query.

"Gina has gone for the day. We don't give out home phone numbers or addresses. You can try reaching her by Twitter. Here's her card."

She had glanced at Garry Davenport and obviously seen an old, grey-haired man. Probably figured him for a geriatric groupie. Thinking about that made him grimace.

He shouldn't have gone in there. It was a telltale sign of his desperation that he had made such a mistake. The only possible saving grace was his age. Young people can't see past grey hair and wrinkles. The receptionist had hardly given him a look.

But he had to be smarter, act smarter. Tomorrow, he would do his homework and determine her schedule. Then next day, he would be there to follow her home.

It was almost a relief when the cellphone rang. Gina had programmed ring tones for all her main contacts. This call was coming from work. She swiftly left Tony's arms to reach for it.

"Sorry to bother you," said Kristen, who worked reception. "I wasn't sure whether to call or not, but—"

"Never worry about bothering me, Kristen. What is it?" Gina asked.

"This creepy guy came in just now and asked about you. He was really old and wanted your phone number. I told him the usual spiel and gave him your Twitter card. But, Gina, this guy was weird."

"Why do you say that?" She could almost hear Kristen shrug.

"Hard to pin down, but he wasn't the type. Had to be over sixty and well-dressed. Not the usual sort to be a fan. And he wouldn't tell me why he wanted you."

Gina watched Tony wander off in the direction of the bathroom. She waited for Kristen to take a breath and continue.

"You know how it is. Sometimes we get people coming here wanting you to appear at charity events and things. Usually they come with an armload of promotional stuff. This guy had nothing, not even a briefcase. But he was wearing an expensive suit."

Gina nodded to herself. Kristen could always pick out people with money. It was a valuable trait in a receptionist...actually, in anybody, even though Tony would poo-poo it.

"And he didn't say what he wanted?"

"Nope. Didn't give his name, either. Ignored me when I asked for it. Maybe he was senile, you know? But it struck me as weird. You might have a crazy fan on your hands."

Gina's heart was picking up speed.

"Thanks, Kristen. It's probably nothing, but I appreciate you giving me a heads-up."

"No probs. Just thought you should know. See you tomorrow." She rang off.

Gina put the cellphone down on the counter. Her heart was beating wildly. This could be the man she had been hoping to trace! Or his representative. He must have seen the article in the paper and found her first.

Of course, maybe she was jumping ahead here. Over half a million people read that paper. Most would have seen that article, and already several media personalities had tried to get in touch with her.

This guy didn't sound like media. And he might just be a lonely older man, a groupie with a bad case of hero-worship, as Kristen had suggested.

Gina had dealt with that kind of problem in the past. It had been so uncomfortable that she had changed her phone number, put it in her mother's name, and ensured it was unlisted. Her mail was forwarded to a box number. The only way strangers could reach her was via her Twitter address and through the station email.

A small part of her mind registered the flush of the toilet and the flow of water from taps.

Should she tell Tony? It took two seconds for her to decide against that. People asked to get in touch with her all the time, through The Weather Network. This could be nothing at all.

Besides, if it really were the man they were looking for, Tony would interfere. He would find all sorts of ways to put a cage around her.

No, it was better to leave things as they were, at least until she had a chance to talk to Becki. She would, of course, tell Becki all about it. Wouldn't she?

Of course she would!

Now was the perfect time. Tony was out for an evening run. He had been sitting too long on the plane, he said. She picked up her phone.

"Hey Bec, how's it going?"

"Oh, I'm glad to hear back from you. Is it awful? The repercussions from the article?"

"Don't know. The PR people are on it. How bad can it be?"

"Just don't want to think you've been made vulnerable somehow."

"On that subject—" Gina twirled her hair with one twitchy finger.

"Oh no! Don't tell me!"

"Okay I won't."

"It's an expression, Gina. Out with it!"

"A strange guy popped into the station this evening asking for me. Wouldn't give his name or why he wanted to see me."

"You didn't go out to meet him did you?"

"I would have but I wasn't there."

"You would have." Disapproval rang in Becki's voice.

"The main lobby is not like some empty dark alley or anything," Gina offered.

"I don't understand you, Gina. You tend to take risks. You worry me."

"No pain no gain."

"Oh that makes me feel a whole lot better!"

"Let me reword that. I mean, if you don't take risks every now and then you don't get ahead. But I haven't told you the best news yet."

"What?"

"Tony's home." The lack of enthusiasm in her voice surprised her.

"That's a relief! Say hi to him for me."

"Will do. He's out for a run right now. It's ironic, but he unwittingly put me onto a new line of thinking with regard to Linda. When he suggested lateral thinking, something flashed across my mind. If Linda/Louisa collected and saved all those fabulous dresses, she absolutely would have saved jewelry to go with them. Accessories make the outfit, right?"

"So where is it? The jewelry to match those dresses? Karl said there was no safety deposit box and we found nothing special during our search."

"Maybe Linda had one of those behind-the-portrait safe deals and we missed it, or maybe she hid it somewhere even more imaginative."

"But why?"

"Those designer dresses were valuable. Can you imagine designer jewelry?"

He should have been home an hour ago. Karl grumbled and felt his stomach rumble in sympathy.

Becki was pretty patient about his job, Karl had to admit. It wasn't so much budget cuts as reluctance on the part of town council to raise taxes to keep up with inflation. In any case, there was a strict moratorium on hiring new staff until the next election. With Jenny out on mat leave, the small department was short-staffed. Karl was working the longer hours, just like everyone else. It was starting to make him weary.

Sergeant Casey popped his head in the doorway.

"Chief, you want to take this call on line two. It's from the sparkies."

Karl nodded and reached for the phone.

"Stevens, that you?"

"Hi, Karl. Look, we found something that might be important to you in that Davidson murder. A strongbox."

Karl looked up in surprise. "Where did you find it?"

"I didn't," said Stevens. "That new fella Miller on the forensic team brought it in. Said it was hidden in the walls of the house, somewhere."

Finally! A break in this otherwise bewildering case. The box might contain papers that would lead to the woman's past.

"Strange, putting it in the wall," Stevens said. "That requires some work. Making a hole between the wood studs, covering it with framed dry wall and then camouflaging it with wallpaper, most likely. Usually people just put their strongboxes in a closet or under a bed."

"She didn't want it found," Karl muttered. *But she also couldn't part with whatever was in it. That made it important.*

"What shape is it in?" he said.

"Singed but intact. I could probably force the lock with a toothpick. You want I should do that now, or should I wait for your guys?"

Karl couldn't wait. He'd known Stevens for years, and trusted the man completely. It wasn't exactly protocol, but he had to know.

"Open it," he said.

Karl could hear the phone being switched to 'Speaker.' The sound of a drawer opening…then the cringe-inducing noise of metal scrapping against metal. More creaks and then a metallic *POP*.

"I'm opening the lid now," said Stevens.

More creaks.

There was a moment of silence. Karl thought he could hear a sudden intake of air.

"Holy shit!"

Karl was out of his chair with the phone at his ear.

"What?"

Stevens was clearly having a hard time talking.

"You're not going to believe this, Karl. Holy crap on a stick."

"What? Spit it out, man!"

Another pause. A bright, tinkling sound traveled through the phone line.

"Your vic must have been the Queen of Sheba or a pirate. I've never seen anything like it. This necklace must be worth a fortune."

Chapter 20

Becki was ready to jump Karl as soon as he got home. Not like *that*. Although that sounded good too.

His shoes thudded on the stairs coming up. He swung open the door. Then he produced that special grin that he never offered anyone else. His eyes lit up with apparent delight to see her although she could tell that he was tired from his slightly stooped posture.

"Hi, hon," he said. "Sorry I'm so late tonight."

She came up to him and kissed him tenderly.

He wrapped his arms around her, both hands pressing on her back, and she did the same but her hands didn't reach nearly as high up on his body.

She was always grateful when he came home at night no matter how late. She rested her head just a little longer against his chest than need be. A cop's wife never takes homecoming for granted. "Hungry?" she asked, pulling away.

"Yeah but I hope you ate," he said. "Hope you didn't wait for me."

"Yeah, I ate." She felt slightly guilty, but it was a deal they had with each other. He didn't want her starving or keeping meals warm in order to accommodate his unpredictable hours. Whenever he could, he let her know well in advance that he was running late, as he did tonight, but even so he was later than expected.

"I'll grab something from the fridge," he said.

Becki knew that on nights like this, he liked to amass a variety of not-so-good-for-you items and just veg out in front of the TV.

And yet the scent of June in Black Currant Bay wafted through the open windows, gently billowing the sheers. Cicadas chirped outside like they were beckoning the two of them to join them on the balcony and chat under the stars instead of holing up inside.

Becki was certain that the magic of moonlight would prove more restful to Karl than artificial blue light from the TV screen.

She convinced him to join her, and out they went together. Becki plopped down in one of the Muskoka chairs and kicked out her legs. Karl arranged his smorgasbord of treats on a patio table and then lowered himself into his own seat, spreading himself out so the tips of his toes almost touched the railing.

They soaked in a night so sensual they could almost taste it.

Ya gotta take advantage of opportunities like this, thought Becki. The older she got the more she realized how precious time like this was.

Eventually, when she saw that Karl was relaxed, she brought up the subject she had been patiently holding in. She knew it wouldn't upset him, just spark some interesting conversation.

"Gina says there has to be some pretty impressive jewelry to go with the dresses we discovered at Louisa's." She didn't mention Louisa's real name. Or what they figured was her real name. "But we didn't find anything when we searched. You didn't either, right? I wonder where it could be."

Karl's eyes widened.

"Tony's home," Becki explained. "He told Gina to think laterally or something and jewels are apparently lateral to dresses." She grinned.

Karl's mouth opened and formed several shapes. His throat worked too, but nothing came out.

"Did I say something wrong?" Becki was suddenly concerned.

"Bingo!"

"Bingo?"

"You hit the jackpot. Louisa had a fire-safe box hidden behind a wall, and when the fire destroyed everything else, it was exposed. You remember Stevens in the fire department? He cracked open the safe while I was on the line and it sounded to me like he couldn't believe his eyes when he looked inside. One stunner of a necklace. I'll see it for myself tomorrow."

In her mind, Becki high-fived Gina. Then something pushed her to ask, "Can I come with you tomorrow?"

"Not necessary, is it?"

Oh but it is! "If you let me come and take pictures of it so I can send them to Gina, I'll tell you what we know about Louisa."

"What do you mean? You've discovered something about Louisa?

"We're not 100 percent sure yet."

"How sure are you?"

"About 99.99 percent?"

"For crying out loud!"

Karl looked severe but she wasn't buying it. Her husband was a softy deep down.

"Do we have a deal?"

"You drive a hard bargain."

Becki explained everything she and Gina had pieced together so far.

Sylvia sat at a table for nine in the glass-fronted Poker Room at Casinoarama. There were twelve tables altogether fairly closely spaced on the rich burgundy carpet and she was at table number one. The other eight players at her table were all male. She knew how ridiculously late it was, but the room was open twenty-four hours a day and as far as she could tell there was always a game on.

She'd started play early in the evening at a lower table and the cards had been in her favour all night so she'd decided to move to the No-limit table.

She peeked at her hole. Out of 52 cards—1,326 distinct possible combinations of two—she had landed a ten of clubs and a ten of diamonds. Luck was still standing by her but she worried that she shouldn't have switched games. She worried but she didn't let it show.

She had to win big tonight to pay down some of her debt before she found herself unable to pay even the interest, because the alternative— bankruptcy—would mean she'd be stuck in dead-end Black Currant Bay forever.

Normally she wouldn't consider losing a cleaning contract pivotal but Louisa had been a very special client, paying bonuses to keep her mouth shut about certain things Sylvia had discovered when she walked in early one day to do her job. Really, Louisa's death was very, very unfortunate and it certainly wasn't something she'd anticipated.

Earlier today she'd read that Becki Green, that woman who owned Beautiful Things, and her friend Gina Monroe from The Weather Network had discovered Louisa's body. Avenues for later?

Not the time to think about that! Focus!

Her eyes itched and burned, her head throbbed and her lower back ached from sitting all this time but she didn't let any of that show either. To the men around the table, only her youth and good looks were on display. Amazing how blind the opposite sex could be. The guys pictured a combination of what they wanted to see and what she wanted them to see.

Small blind, big blind, bets around the table clockwise round and round, two players out, the dealer burns a card, three-card flop face-up, no ten.

The dealer burns another card, the turn is dealt, no ten.

Odds in my head, chips dwindling, the dealer burns the last card of the hand, finally the river, it's a ten.
All in...

Chapter 21

Cathy stared at the photo, the one personal likeness she had of Garry Davenport. It had been taken over twenty years ago, on a weekend away at the very beginning of their affair, when they had both been madly in love with each other, and strangely addicted to the risk.

Garry stood on the balcony of their second-floor room at an exclusive Muskoka resort. He had been standing casually, looking out across the cobalt lake, when she had called his name. His head turned in response, and she caught him on camera just before he smiled.

Her heart still tugged when she looked down at the photo. The wisps of memory were becoming stronger. This man had been the love of her life. There had been no one before or after that had made her heart sing like Garry. She was pretty sure she had been the same to him. Heartbreak—the resulting heartbreak from the trial and her own slinking back to the shadows—was something that haunted her to this day.

Their relationship had never ended. They had never 'broken up.' She had simply stayed in the shadows as he lived out his sentence in prison. As her own marriage became quietly unglued, she continued to stay in the shadows.

This had been his wish.

She looked down at the masculine face in the photo.

Never a word from him. Not one word since the day he was arrested. That was the thing. If he'd written to her *just once…* Was he still protecting her? Could there still be danger for her?

Cathy was almost positive it was protection that was keeping him silent. That would be in character. But the mind has a way of doubting itself after the passing of many years.

Cathy didn't regret those months long ago. The years in between had been painful, but she had lived an opera. She had *lived.* So much better to look back on life and think, *I have experienced the kind of passion that very few are fortunate to have in a lifetime.*

Yes, it was worth it, a thousand times worth it. And it would be worth it again. She would do it all again—everything. She put the photo down on the glass coffee table and picked up the phone.

It was a dream come true. Sylvia could hardly contain her excitement.

The elderly man in the cashier booth gave her a crooked tooth smile.

"Gonna go on a world cruise?" he said. "You can smuggle me aboard in a suitcase."

Sylvia hooted. The idea of her hooking up with this geezer—which usually would have had her turning up her lip in a snarl—now seemed hilarious. *So that was what money could do for you. It put you in a totally different frame of mind.*

"Pay off some debts," she said. "And maybe buy a new car. One of those cute sporty convertibles, you know? I've always wanted one."

She was floating on a cloud, she was. Did rich people feel this way all the time? Or did they get used to it?

"You were smart to stop when you did. Most people blow their chance by getting too greedy." The old man handed her a slip.

Sylvia nodded in agreement. For once, she had done things right. Held back. Taken the winnings. Not pushed her luck.

She wandered out to the parking lot in a state of euphoria. What would she do first? Should she stop cleaning houses? Cancel her customers?

Go on a trip? Buy a car?

She couldn't do everything, of course. There wasn't *that* much money. Maybe...keep the customers she had, keep cleaning, and live high for a while. Get the hot car. Go to Bermuda or Mexico. Buy some great clothes and stuff.

She unlocked the door to her beat-up Ford Focus, head filled with grand plans.

Becki stared at the jeweled necklace on the battered precinct desk.

"I waited until everyone left for the day before calling you. Didn't want to explain why you were...well, you know what I mean. Easier this way," Karl said.

Becki smiled and nodded. Karl wouldn't want to admit his wife was helping with the case, no matter how little she was. It wasn't just pride. There were unspoken rules about outsiders.

The necklace certainly was a stunner. The gems were set in white gold. They sparkled royal blue and shiny white under the florescent lights. There were earrings to match for pierced ears—drop things, very blingy. The stones were too large to be real.

"Pretty baubles, aren't they?" Karl stood beside her. "Sort of like the crown jewels."

"They would match that dress we found, for sure," Becki said. "I expect they were created for each other. Designers do that. May I touch them?"

Karl shrugged. "Sure."

Becki reached forward with both hands. She felt Karl watching her carefully. He had a frown on his face. Was he regretting that he hadn't thought to buy her pretty jewelry like this? Not that they ever went anywhere you could wear something so ornate.

But Becki had more important things to think about. Maybe she could find a brand name. She turned over the necklace and scrutinized the area where Gina had trained her to look. *No hope of it.*

"Hand me your reading glasses," she said to Karl.

He passed them to her. They were ridiculously large on her nose, and even more powerful than her own, which would still be lying where she had forgotten them, on the bedside table.

Becki looked again at the markings on the back of the clasp.

Her head snapped up. She put the necklace down and turned to Karl. "I need to call Gina."

Karl nodded, but looked surprised. He handed Becki the handset of his desk phone.

Gina answered on the first ring. Becki explained where she was, and why.

"I'm taking a photo and sending it to you. Ring me back on this line when you get it," Becki said.

She hung up. "You don't mind if I take a photo of these, right? It's only for Gina. She won't show it around."

Karl raised an eyebrow. "Okay. Tell her to keep it confidential. What are you cooking up between the two of you?"

Becki smiled, but didn't answer. She removed the cellphone from her purse and got busy with her task.

A few minutes later, the desk phone rang. Becki picked it up, listened and then answered.

"Says 18 K."

She listened again, and her eyes went wide. She covered the speaker with her other hand and turned to Karl.

"Gina says it's real."

"What?" Karl exclaimed.

"She says designers don't set costume jewelry in 18 karat gold. That's what I was checking on the back of the clasp. It says the setting is 18 K. Gina says those rhinestones are actually diamonds, and the blue stones will be sapphires."

They stared at each other in shock.

Becki turned her attention to the phone in her hand. "Here—I'm putting the receiver down and turning the phone on speaker, Gina. How much would they be worth, do you think?"

Gina's silky television voice came through clearly on the speakerphone. "Three, four hundred thousand, probably. I once saw a set in Bulgari like that, but the stones weren't as big. They were $365,000 US. So maybe more. It would depend on the quality."

"What did you call that type of stone? Sapphire? I thought sapphires were small." Karl was scratching his head.

"That's why they don't look real," Gina said. "But they're real all right, although rare. I'd bet my engagement ring."

No you wouldn't, thought Becki.

"So do you think this is what the arsonist was looking for, Karl?" Gina asked.

"Could be," Karl said thoughtfully. "Thing is, they were hidden in a wall. Who would even know she had these?"

It was nearly an hour later when Cathy put down the phone. First, she had tried to reach Gina, but that line was busy. Next, she tried Gina's mother. That had led to a half hour discussion about the arrangements for the hospital fundraising ball, and Cathy's part in arranging the entertainment.

Following that, she had phoned the magician to confirm his arrival time and hours of duty. He would go from table to table entertaining patrons, while the band took breaks. In all, she thought the guests would get value for their high-priced tickets. At one thousand dollars a plate, and ten thousand a table, this was definitely a high-priced affair.

No matter. They never had trouble filling the seats in a city as big as Toronto. It was an excuse to see and be seen, to show off acquired wealth, more than anything else.

But all for a good cause, as Anna continually reminded. That was true. This time, the hospital would get needed medical equipment, like a new MRI.

Cathy didn't work at a job. She didn't have kids to raise anymore. You needed to do something with your time besides shop and lunch. Charity event planning was the one thing she could do well, that actually did some good. Also, she liked the women who did this. They were amazingly competent for being stay-at-home wives.

She got up from the couch and wandered into the kitchen, with thoughts about dinner. As she gazed into the sub-zero fridge, the doorbell rang.

Cathy closed the fridge door, hoping wildly for the pizza man. That's what she wanted tonight—pizza. Maybe he read her mind and was already there?

She flung open the front door, shaking her head with a silly smile on her face.

It vanished immediately.

"You?" she said, with a choked hush.

"Hello, Cathy. You've hardly changed at all. May I come in?" said Garry Davenport.

Chapter 22

Cathy had hesitated for a split second. And then she threw herself into Garry's arms, nearly knocking him off the stoop. For a moment they clung there, oblivious to the moments passing. And then Garry had released his relentless hold, pushed back to gaze at her, and kissed her face in a dozen places.

That had been two hours ago. Now, after the tears, the awkward first words, the urgent passion to become reacquainted with each other's bodies after so long, they lay content in her bed, in each other's arms. Cathy had to wonder that it seemed so right, and so natural.

"I dreamed of this for years and years," muttered Garry.

Cathy sighed with contentment. She wanted to ask—oh how she wanted to ask—if she had been his last lover. But she held her tongue, so as not to spoil the moment.

"Not too rusty, I hope?" he ventured.

Cathy giggled. Now she had her answer, and it filled her with joy.

"No rust on that steel. And no need for Viagra," she said.

He laughed. "No, no need for that. I've been saving up a long, long time, sweet thing." He kissed her shoulder. "I swear you are sexier now than back in those days."

"Hardly that," she murmured. "I wanted to contact you so badly. So many times, I nearly did."

"I knew that. I also knew that you would stay hidden. You'd understand my wishes and respect them."

Yes, she had gotten that. His lack of communication with her had been a deliberate sign for her to stay out of the picture. She knew him well enough to know that. Even though it hurt like hell. Even though she knew it was for her own sake. And safety.

"What will you do now?"

He moved to sit up. "I'm not sure. Would you mind having a man in the house for the time being?"

Her heart leaped with joy, but her mind was playful.

"What makes you think there isn't one already?"

He smiled down at her. It was an odd smile...not conveying happiness so much as shrewd satisfaction. "There isn't. I know. I've known everything you've ever done from the moment I went in, Cath."

Her first thought was, *how?* And then she remembered. Garry was well-connected. He was also a master businessman. He would have organized everything he wanted to keep track of well before entering prison, and hired the people to do it. Hell—he probably was able to keep organizing everything while he was *in* prison. He was just that sort of guy.

There was no doubt in her mind Garry had shady connections. That had come out during the trial. But even before, she had known. It even— if she was being honest with herself—made him more exciting, back then.

So Garry had been keeping track of her...had even hired people to do it.

Good thing her life had been sort of blameless since the divorce. Really, there had only been a couple of tepid dates that went nowhere. Because beneath everything, Cathy couldn't rid herself of her longing for this one man.

No one else would do.

"So. What have you got planned for the next while?" Garry asked.

"Just some charity functions. What did you have in mind?"

Garry rose from the bed. She watched him stretch, his body still lean and hard from physical activity. It made a contrast to his face, which was heavily lined and showed his age.

"I have a few loose ends to clear up. Financial stuff."

Oh dear. Financial stuff. For years, Cathy had wondered where the money had all gone. Garry had been one of the super-rich, super-elite in Toronto. Not only did he live on the Bridal Path, he was a member of the Granite Club, and also the Royal Canadian Yacht Club.

Money had been an issue at the trial, of course. A whole bunch was missing. Shareholders were up in arms. Words like 'swindled' peppered the papers.

The monster house and Muskoka cottage had been sold when Garry went to prison. But where had all that money gone?

Cathy rose from the bed and reached for her aqua dressing gown on the antique chair beside the bed.

"Anything I can help with?"

"Don't worry about money, sweetheart. I won't have to freeload off you. I have some tucked away. And a lot more coming, when I can get at it."

He sat back on the bed to pull on his pants.

"First thing. I have to get a hold of this woman who may be able to give me some information."

Cath tensed instinctively at the words 'this woman.' Last thing she wanted was another woman in the picture. "Who is it?"

"Gina something. She's on The Weather Network." Garry rose from the bed and did up his zipper.

"Gina Monroe?" Cathy could hardly believe it.

"That's the name. I tried to see her at the studio, but no go. They locked up tight. It's like she's a major celebrity or something and they're keeping out the paparazzi."

"But I know her! She's the daughter of a friend. I had dinner with her just this week."

Garry swung around, startled. "You know Gina Monroe?"

Cathy nodded. "And she'll see you if I ask her to."

Garry moved across the floor and gathered her up in his arms.

"Did I ever tell you, you're the answer to a prayer?"

The smell of his musky scent engulfed her body in a euphoric haze.

So this is joy, she thought. *Way beyond happiness.*

And she would do everything possible to keep it going.

A new day was starting up in Black Currant Bay. Becki and Gina had been chatting on the phone for 15 minutes and had discussed Tony's attitude, the upcoming wedding, and now Becki brought up the subject of Louisa's murder and what they had been doing to try and shed some light on it.

"One thing I've heard from Karl throughout the years is that in 97% of cases, the suspect is mentioned at some point during the first 30 days of the investigation," Becki said. She squeezed several of the fat spirals of the landline's cord between her fingers.

"Hasn't been thirty days," Gina pointed out.

"No."

"What has it been?"

"Half that. Almost two weeks?"

"Wow. Time flies."

"You're telling me." Becki gave a great sigh. "We found Louisa just a couple days before your shower."

There was a long pause while they both remembered.

Gina said, "I bet the theory works as well within a two-week period. I bet we *have* come across the killer."

"Creepy, huh?"

"Yes, but maybe we can do something about it," Gina suggested. "Maybe we can help piece together the puzzle. They say two minds are better than one. How about the more minds the merrier?"

"I guess we could at least make a list of suspects." Becki was an organized sort of person. Since she had called Gina from her desk at Beautiful Things, it was easy to grab an always nearby notepad and pencil. "I'll write it down," she offered.

"Who were the first people we encountered?" Gina began. "The cops. Do we count them or are they exempt?"

"Exempt I should think. But let's cast a large web and then narrow it down."

"Actually, it was the ambulance guys that came in first."

"And then Karl…"

"You're not writing him on the list!"

"Nah," Becki said. "Because if we put him on the list, we'd have to put ourselves on it too."

"Let's not get ridiculous."

"We spotted that guy skulking around Louisa's house," Becki recalled.

"Douglas Spellman, the developer."

"Who else shows up on your radar in connection with Louisa?" Becki asked.

"Weather reference?"

"Couldn't pass it up."

"Lottie then. She's on my radar."

"Louisa's friend. The one she was going to take to Cornwall."

"If we can believe what Lottie says, that is. She's a little dotty, don't you think? Sees ghosts. They speak to her, she claims."

"Don't write her off so quickly," Becki said. "After all, I talk to my dead mom."

"But the poor woman doesn't talk back."

Becki held back the whole truth of the matter.

"Then there's Garry Davenport, Louisa's ex, the entertainment mogul," Gina continued. "Maybe through him, Louisa even had some knowledge that was dangerous to the mob. Put 'mob' on your list."

"And what about your mother's friend, Cathy? Davenport's mistress?"

"Put her down. She couldn't have burned down Louisa's house personally because she was with me but...um...you never know, do you?"

"The only other person I can think of that we've discovered in connection to Louisa is Sylvia."

"Who's she again?"

"Louisa's cleaning lady."

"Right. Louisa didn't seem to have much in the way of friends and family that could inherit, did she?"

"I guess she was kind of like a recluse." Becki read off the list.

ambulance crew
2 police officers
developer—Douglas Spellman
Lottie
entertainment mogul—Garry Davenport
mob
Cathy
Sylvia

"Not a very long list," Gina said.

Chapter 23

Oh, yeah! What a fabulous day!

High on endorphins from winning big just days before, and euphoric about yesterday's purchase of a 2014 MINI Cooper S Convertible —built from scratch just the way she wanted it and to be delivered within the week—Sylvia skipped up Main Street.

A Midnight Black Metallic 2014 MINI Cooper S Convertible to be specific! She pictured herself stepping out of her brand new wheels wearing a slinky black dress to match the paint, and atop glittery platform shoes. Just in front of the trendiest dance club in Toronto.

She'd shared her wonderful news, her vision of the future, as well as plenty of cash, in local stores all the way from the lake to the subdivision marking the end of the commercial district. Everyone was so happy for her! Store clerks. Clients. Regular Black Currant Bay shoppers. Heck, even summer tourists. True, the visitors to town tended to look at her peculiarly when she admitted her goal was to make enough money to move away permanently.

Oh but right now she felt as gloriously radiant as the sun! Her limbs threatened to break into dance of their own accord.

About one quarter up the grade leading to her low-rise apartment building, however, her loaded paper shopping bags started to drag her down just a teeny bit. She rebalanced them in two hands and continued on.

Nah, nothing can stop me from soaring into high-rise condo airspace! And it will be soon, because all my recent efforts on several fronts have paid off beautifully.

She would continue her upward climb. Even if most people she'd confided in about her varied projects didn't understand or approve.

My time listening to sceptical naysayers and their judgemental lectures about my money-making methods is so last year.

Ouch! The multi-coloured cords and ribbons of the bags were cutting right into her flesh. Perhaps in her excitement she had purchased just a little too much stuff at the same time.

Here, about halfway up the hill, lots were very wide and long. Trees stately. The traffic calm to non-existent.

She set down her packages on the smooth cement sidewalk to rearrange them once again. Not much further now and she would be flying up the few stairs outside her home at the edge of town. She would surge past door number 1A, then she would unwrap all her splendid items. She'd admire the décor pieces in several different spots around her apartment until she found just the right one. She'd check out how she looked in her new clothes in all her mirrors.

Bending over to pick up her packages again, she looked up in the direction she was headed, more determined than ever to traverse the remaining blocks with no more stops.

A dark sedan drove toward her. *Nice,* she thought. But nothing like the compact gem of a vehicle she'd chosen at the dealership.

Weird. The car seems to be speeding up. Um...down. Down the hill.

Automatically she checked the driver behind the wheel of the increasingly fast-moving vehicle.

Is there a problem?

Sylvia's expertise in observation served her just as well in everyday matters as in gambling, which is all about reading people's tells.

Facial expression.

Body language.

No mystery to her—

Then her bags slipped from her hands.

The car was almost upon her.

No mistaking the expression in the sedan driver's stare.

She had miscalculated.

For the first time since she could remember, fear crept into her consciousness. Her breathing came in short pants past her lips. Her mind raced.

The wheels of the car bounced up over the curb.

Don't panic. Play your hand. Fifty-fifty chance. Should I leap left or right?

Sylvia was a gambler.

She bet left.

Becki was taking a break from work. Fresh air and exercise were important parts of her life in Black Currant Bay so instead of grabbing a coffee and sitting somewhere and relaxing like most city workers would do, she had flung open the front door of Beautiful Things and headed north.

Up Main Street this time, not down to the lake. Uphill all the way. She would turn around where the road levelled off and then, before heading back down, she'd take in the panorama of the semi-circle of town hugging the isolated shore of Lake Huron's Georgian Bay.

Lake Ontario was her favourite Great Lake because she grew up in Toronto, but she remembered that in school she'd been fascinated by all five of the Great Lakes, including Lake Huron. She distinctly remembered colouring inside the mapped lake borders in blue pencil crayon.

High up at this end of town, there was more breeze and there were fewer people. The only other person she could see ahead was a lone woman, weighed down with bags in both hands and walking like maybe she was tired, and wearing uncomfortable shoes.

Whoa!

What's going on?

A dark car streaked down the hill at an angle that would have him hitting the curb vis-à-vis where the woman was walking.

"Watch out!" Becki cried.

Horrified, she saw the woman try to leap out of the way but she was hit.

Thrown like a rag doll.

She lay crumpled on the strip of grass between the sidewalk and the road.

And the car kept coming.

Instinct insisted Becki take cover.

A nearby maple with a trunk nearly three feet in diameter would protect her from this maniac, who had careened across the road, mounted the sidewalk, mowed down a pedestrian, never stopping.

His full-size, luxury vehicle, dark blue with a silvery quality, flashed by and Becki drilled her eyes at the spot where the license plate should be, willing herself to record the letters and numbers, but the car sped away too quickly.

The front tire's missing a hub cap thingy. It'll be up near the scene.

She slipped out from behind the tree and ran as fast as she could to assist the victim.

Many miles away, a man worried about another woman.

Tony was not happy. It was happening again, and he seemed powerless to stop it.

Why couldn't Gina leave this small-town murder alone? Why did she and Becki insist on trying to solve a killing that even the experts were struggling with?

Sure, they were smart. They'd probably solve the thing, if given half a chance. But at what risk?

It was dangerous and foolhardy. You didn't poke a snake. The murderer was still out there, and it didn't take a government agent to figure out that a deadly snake might strike again, if threatened.

Nobody was more dangerous than a human who had already killed. He knew that from experience.

Tony drummed his fingers on the steering wheel of his late-model sports car. Gina wouldn't thank him for interfering. But he didn't have time to guard the ladies, as they played Sherlock. Not with the other pressing thing on his agenda.

The irony of this situation was not lost on him. Gina worried constantly about his safety while performing his 'other' job, the one he was leaving right before the wedding. Now, Tony was in the panic seat, over her.

It had come to a crescendo earlier today in the condo. Tony had entered quietly, as was his habit and training. He stood there, frozen in the foyer, as Gina put down the phone.

Gina turned around and started. No other word for it. She looked guilty.

"I didn't see you there. When did you come in?"

He stared back at her, leaning back against the door with his arms crossed. "A few minutes ago. Long enough to figure out you were talking with Becki about that murder."

Gina turned away. She walked into the living room and started tidying up the newspaper sections that littered the coffee table.

"We were just discussing who might be suspects."

"I heard you," said Tony. "Does Karl know you're still at it?"

Gina's hands shifted from neatening up newspapers to adjusting pillows on the sofa.

"At what?" she said.

Tony cursed under his breath. "Don't be coy, Gina. It's obvious you two are still playing Nancy Drew."

He could see her flinch with anger at the childish reference.

"We're not 'playing.' I found out who the victim was, remember? I was the one who made the connection, and we gave it to the police."

And the conversation just went downhill from there.

Mere minutes later, he had walked out of the condo to cool off.

What to do? Put a tail on them? He could do that. H certainly had the contacts. But would it do any good*? Might be too much, too late. You can't stop a murderer intent on killing. You simply can't be everywhere, and in a position to stop violence from a distance.* He knew that from experience too.

Tony cursed. It wasn't like him to ask for help, but this involved more than just Gina, and he was sure the other guy would be just as concerned.

Karl answered on the second ring, tension clear in his voice.

Tony got right to the point.

"They're still investigating that damned woman's death, did you know?"

This time, Karl cursed. "I can't talk now. There's been another attempted murder."

Part II

Chapter 24

Roles had switched. Becki was not Gina's host in Black Currant Bay. She was Gina's guest in Toronto.

Tony had retreated to his bachelor pad for the final week before the wedding.

It was Saturday noon and the girls would have been sitting outside on a restaurant patio for lunch except the heat was so brutal they'd asked for a table inside instead.

That old expression "so hot, you could fry an egg on the sidewalk" is not hyperbole, Becki thought as a determined bead of sweat trickled down her back.

She knew this because she had once looked it up on the Net.

Anal of me to fact-check something like that, she admitted to herself. *But hey, next time the subject comes up I won't have to be concerned about making exaggerated and unverified statements. Except of course I've never actually fried an egg on the sidewalk myself, have I? I'm still taking someone else's word for it. But I can trust Bill Nye the Science Guy, right?*

It was he who confirmed that, indeed, sidewalks can be hotter than air temperatures because they are not only heated by air convection but by the sun's radiation as well.

And right now the sun blistered a cityscape that was wall to wall man-made elements like cement, asphalt, brick and glass. Natural vegetation was limited to dwarf trees—strictly decorative—bordering the sidewalk, a few planters of flowers along patio railings and some giant potted arrangements in front of trendy store entrances.

The natural elements are hardly proportional, she thought. *OMG! Here I am trying to redesign Toronto. This heat must be affecting me. For example, how many times have I re-read this same menu section?*

She tapped it with her forefinger to help with concentration. It's not like the offerings didn't interest her. In fact, Gina was indulging her and had suggested a meal here at Rawlicious, where everything on the menu was both vegan and raw.

Two steps beyond her vegetarianism. And utterly intriguing.

For example, apparently the underlying principle behind raw was the conservation of vitamins, minerals and especially digestive-friendly enzymes by not heating food above 118°F.

Better not let the food touch the sidewalk, she mused.

Gina's voice cut through the haze of heat and the drone of noise. "What are you getting?"

The floor to ceiling windows in the front were open to the street so there was no air conditioning happening. *Get it together, Becki. Pick something and...and answer Gina's question.* "Hmm. Chocolate Nut Milk and...um...Pad Thai, I think. You?"

"I wonder what the Creamsicle Smoothie would be like. Remember Creamsicles? When I was little I used to ride my bike to the corner store and that's what I'd buy."

And now she's getting married. In one week. "Yeah. At one time they were my favourite frozen treat too. Then I went on a Fudgsicle binge. Anyway, nutmilk, banana, avocado, orange, vanilla, agave. Sounds delicious."

"I'll try it with Spring Rolls. If I'm still hungry I'll have dessert."

They placed their orders and chatted about nothing and everything until the food arrived. It was delivered by a friendly waiter and they both found their dishes well-presented and tasty. Filling too. Not surprising as there were no animal products in any of the items, which meant plenty of fibre in all of them.

Maybe nourishing food was all Becki needed after her long drive from Black Currant Bay this morning. Once they'd finished eating she felt re-energized. Which was a good thing because this afternoon they were going for the final fitting of Becki's maid-of-honour gown.

Even if the wedding was going to be quite the grand gathering, there would be only two attendants in the bridal party. Becki, as more of a witness, really, than virginal maid of honour, and one of Tony's friends as his witness/best man.

Becki picked up her purse because she knew their appointment loomed. She dug out her wallet and paid the tab for both of them. After all, Gina was letting her stay at the condo. She added a generous tip and was about to get up when Gina said, "Before we go, I want to give you something."

"You do?" It should be she who was handing over a sweet little box embellished with polka-dot trim to the bride to be.

Gina's wedding gift will come later, Becki consoled herself. *And Gina and Tony will open it after their honeymoon.*

"Open it now!" The future bride's eyes danced like those of a child offering a valentine heart made of doilies.

Becki tugged on the two ends of the ribbon and the bow dissolved into swirling lengths of satin on the table. Slowly she lifted the cardboard lid, spread the glittery tissue and revealed...a stunning neckpiece.

"It will go with your dress," Gina said. "I know you love vintage."

Pieces of turquoise in a filigree-like pattern of silver. It was gorgeous, and statement necklaces were so in style these days.

"Oh my! Lovely! Spectacular!" Becki did get up from her chair then and came around and hugged Gina tightly. "Thank you so, so much!"

"It's for being by my side on the most important day of my life."

Becki had to sit down again for the emotion. "Wow, thank you so much!" she said again. She had to clear her throat. "It's totally my privilege, Gina. I wouldn't be anywhere else for the world. On the day of your wedding I'll wear your gift with the greatest pride. And I'll treasure it forever because it's from you and will be a reminder of your special day. Moreover, my dear..." She couldn't not say it. "...this is one killer necklace!"

Sylvia's eyes darted around the room. A curtain of faded green, peach and mauve stripes at the side of her bed was pushed back to reveal insipid green hospital walls.

She blinked again. Definitely a hospital. From this position lying on her back, she could see the shabby grey-white acoustic ceiling tiles disappear around the corner.

It was quiet. The door to the room must have been closed. She tried to lift her head to see better.

Ouch! Not happening.

Sylvia relaxed back into the pillow, and tried to think.

The car coming at her. The determined face. She had dodged left.

Had it been the right choice?

She was alive. *That's what counted.*

Sylvia tried to take stock. Her neck had hurt when she tried to rise up. *Bugger.*

Her left arm appeared to be okay. She could move it, and the hand. Her right arm was in a sling.

Her right leg was heavy. It appeared to be encased in plaster.

Shit. How am I going to get anything done with a cast?

Her head hurt too, just a dull ache. She put her good hand up to her forehead and felt along there. *At least her hair was still there.*

A metallic clunk broke the silence. The door swung open. Someone was coming into the room. Instinctively, Sylvia tensed.

Not a killer—a policeman.

Sylvia relaxed a bit. But not totally.

The man at the foot of her bed was a well-known face around town. He was the police chief, she knew. Even though he was probably over fifty, she instinctively reached up to check her hair. *A good-looking man was a good-looking man, whatever the age, and you can't fight biology.*

The frown on his face smoothed away when he saw she was awake.

"Good," he said, in a low masculine voice. "You're back with us."

He reached over, and with a big square hand, moved the plastic guest chair into position so he could sit on it. The chair rocked with his body.

"My name is Karl. I'm a policeman. Do you know where you are?"

Sylvia remembered the neck pain just in time. Instead of nodding, she spoke. "In the hospital."

Gad, her voice sounded strange…like it was underwater.

The big policeman nodded. "Do you remember why?"

Should she tell the truth? Sylvia rarely told the truth.

Okay, that isn't quite true. It's just that she didn't tell the truth without thinking about it beforehand.

And right now, she couldn't think of a good reason not to tell the truth.

"A car hit me."

That seemed to satisfy the policeman. He nodded and leaned forward.

"Did you see who was driving the car? Was it anyone you recognized?"

Now she hesitated. She tried to look thoughtful.

"No. It all happened so quickly. I saw it coming and I tried to get out of the way."

He was staring at her now, really making her uncomfortable.

"Did you happen to catch any of the license plate?"

She shook her head, and immediately flinched from the pain. It must have shown on her face, because the policeman snapped out of his hard look.

"I know you're in pain. This won't take long. I just need to find out if you can help us find the person who did this to you."

Ice water couldn't make her feel colder. Now she knew it was deliberate, for sure.

"So…it wasn't an accident?" Her voice was a harsh whisper.

The big man looked away. "We have a witness who says the car went right for you. Have you any idea who would want to do something like that?"

Shit, shit, shit. Of course she knew. She just couldn't believe it. Well, she didn't know for sure, of course, because the car windows were tinted. There definitely were a few contenders, some more probable than others.

It's just that she couldn't believe anyone would go to this length.

Her business had been mildly lucrative, and seemingly *safe*. Secrets were worth money. A little here, a little there. Not enough to cause this sort of reaction.

The policeman was waiting.

Sylvia cleared her throat. "I can't imagine. I'm just a person who cleans houses."

She tried to sound helpless and simple. It usually worked with men, and Sylvia had perfected the technique. But then, she suddenly had the most brilliant, clever thought. Something that would put him right off the obvious track.

She shifted her eyes over to his and opened them wide.

"Do you think it has anything to do with that poor murdered woman? I used to clean her house."

She watched his face consider it, looking for some sign that he was buying her act. It was hard to tell. He looked weary, that's what he looked. *A good sign.*

She congratulated herself on so cleverly throwing him off the scent, and tried one more thing.

"Is it," she managed a little gasp, "an insane person? A serial killer?"

Karl rose slowly from the chair. "We're considering everything. I'll be back to see you tomorrow. Rest well."

I'll try, she said to herself. *But it's going to be hard what with someone wanting me dead and all.*

The doorbell wouldn't stop ringing. Garry Davenport cursed. Why the hell Cathy had to go to the hairdresser…

Now the door was being pounded out of the wall.

He charged down the length of the hall and flung open the wooden door.

"Hello, Mr. Davenport."

Garry felt the air being sucked from his lungs.

On the step was a short, dark-haired man in a charcoal grey suit with no tie. The fabric strained over his arms. He looked like a boxer. His nose had been broken at least once.

He wasn't a stranger.

Garry watched his face. There were deep lines now, where there hadn't been years before, but he still had that thick head of hair. *Lucky bastard.*

"Johnny," Garry said, holding the door firm. He didn't invite the man in.

"Nice to see you're out." The younger man reached into his pocket.

For one brief moment, Garry thought he was done for.

But Johnny's hand came out with an envelope, not a gun.

"My boss would like to meet with you. To welcome you back, like. Here's where and when." He handed the letter to Garry.

Garry took it and continued to stare at it. He felt glued to the ground, unable to move.

"Oh. A word of advice. You don't want to miss this meeting," Johnny said. "Wouldn't be polite." He smiled with a lot of small white teeth.

"Have a nice day." He turned and sauntered off the porch, down the flagstone steps to the road. Parked there was a black, late model Mercedes.

When had they started driving Mercs? Garry wondered. *In the old days, it had been Cadillacs. Damned unpatriotic, not supporting our industry.*

He watched the sedan pull away from the curb. Then he re-entered the house and locked the door behind him.

His heart was still racing.

So they had found him. It wasn't enough to hide out at Cathy's. They could obviously find him anywhere in the city.

He looked down at the envelope in his hand like it contained poison.

He wasn't safe here. Worse, Cathy wasn't safe here. If they couldn't get to him, they would get to Cathy.

Hot sweat oozed from every gland.

He had to get Cathy away from here.

Chapter 25

According to Gina, if they wanted to make it to St. Francis of Assisi in Little Italy by 11:30 they really had to boogie.

Sunday brunch dishes hastily piled on the counter, they grabbed their purses and dashed from the condo, Gina locking the door quickly behind them.

The elevator brought them smoothly down to street level. A few more steps and a swoosh through the rotating front door of the building and they passed from acclimatized and shady interior to humid and brilliant exterior. A little ducking and weaving allowed them to slip into the throngs of other people doing their thing already on Yonge.

While keeping pace with Gina, Becki marvelled at her surroundings and compared them to her adopted home up north. *Black Currant Bay is like traditional, block-printed wallpaper in the most simple of patterns and a couple complimentary colours. Charming. Serene.*

Toronto is like avant-garde, freehand paper of intricate design with full-spectrum colour. Fascinating. Exuberant.

She would have loved to stay above-ground but the first leg of their trip was to be by subway. The underbelly. Greyer. Damper. Colder.

Too many other jostling commuters to get a seat so it wasn't a good time to talk.

They exited at College Station and transferred to WEST—506 CARLTON toward HIGH PARK. Streetcar. It had been a long time since Becki rode the Rocket! Where did the dreadful screeching come from exactly? The wheels on the tracks or the pole on the electric lines? Karl would know.

Through the windows of the lurching vehicle, Becki watched the community change from block to block. That was another neat thing about Toronto. It never stayed the same.

"We're almost there," Gina said, getting up just before their stop.

The doors opened for them and they hopped off at College and Grace.

"Not too far now."

"Oh don't worry about me. I walk all over the place in Black Currant Bay."

"Can't wait for you to see it. I think it's beautiful. St. Francis has been our family church for forever." Gina winked. "Maybe I should have brought you to the 9:00 mass. All in Italian."

As they walked south on Grace, a street of older homes and mature trees, a square church tower beckoned on the left.

"Tell me what you think," Gina said when they stood right in front.

"Ah, it *is* beautiful, Gina. A romantic place to be married for sure. I do love stone." She was quiet for a moment. "Gothic Revival."

"Only you would know that. All I know is it was finished in 1915 and has 21 stained glass windows."

"I love stained glass windows."

"Come on in."

Lottie grasped the necklace as if it were a rosary. The cross with eleven purple stones dangled from its solid gold chain, trapped between crooked fingers. But instead of counting and praying, she worried the strand.

"Louisa," she moaned. "My friend, how can I make you understand? How can I explain myself to a ghost?"

She rocked, and as she rocked she twisted the necklace. She couldn't sit still.

"It's Sunday today, Louisa. It's less than a week until my young friend Gina gets married. St. Francis of Assisi. She told us that. Wasn't it a lovely shower?

"Oh yes. Such a doll Gina is. A celebrity too. We're fast friends now, you know. Gina invited me to her wedding.

"And I want to go, Louisa. So you mustn't say anything at all to her."

While Gina was talking to some folks she knew, Becki dropped coins into the proper box and then lit a candle for Gina and Tony and their future happiness. She loved the symbolism of a flame burning in a church in support of love.

When Gina was ready to go, Becki suggested, "Let's cross the street to that park and sit for just a bit before we head back. It's such a lovely day."

"Are you hungry?" Gina asked.

"No, not yet."

"'Cause we could get a gelato. This is the right neighbourhood."

They strolled to a bench under the dappled shade of a big old maple. It reminded Becki of the maple behind Godmother's house. Gina's deceased grandmother. *Let's not go there.*

When they were settled and doing nothing more than watching park pigeons poke for crumbs or bugs or whatever pigeons typically scrounged for, Becki said quietly, "There's something wrong, isn't there, Gina?"

Gina looked at her hands. "You noticed?"

"Of course I noticed."

Then Gina sighed.

"Do you want to tell me?"

"No."

"But you will, right? Get it off your chest? Maybe I can help. If not me, your mother?"

"No. You."

Becki waited patiently. She'd pushed enough already.

"Remember when Tony called before the shower and said he was going to Montreal?"

"Yeah."

"That…that job of his is an issue with us still. There's still tension."

"I'm sorry." *That's the first thing to say.*

For a marriage to work the bride and groom must begin head over heels in love with each other. No doubts, thought Becki. *When that's the case then there's a right decision to look back on.*

Unfortunately, from her experience, when a couple started off with doubts it inevitably ended in disaster.

"I don't think he's going to stop all his spy stuff even if he says he is," Gina explained.

"And you want him to stop because you worry about him."

"There are occupational hazards."

"More than…"

"More than when you're an architect."

"Such as."

"Such as he'll be gone all the time."

"You'll miss him."

"And he could get killed."

"You love him."

"And there are the secrets."

"Don't you trust him?"

"Of course I trust him."

Becki remained silent. The leaves rustled in the trees above. The patterns changed on the ground. The pigeons pecked.

"No, I don't trust him."

"Did he ever give you reason not to trust him?"

"Like what?"

"Has he ever really lied to you, Gina? As opposed to just not telling you the whole story?"

"That's the thing. Not telling the whole story seems like lying to me. I'm a reporter. What if I reported only half the news? 'Sun, sun, sun,' for instance, and neglected to add, 'until midday when a tornado will swoop down.'"

God, relationships are complicated!

At one point Becki herself had been tempted to discount marriage. With a fifty percent failure rate, who would not challenge wedlock as an out-dated model? Oprah Winfrey seemed happy as a lark as a monogamous but unwed partner.

But then she got to thinking that it's not the institution that's corrupt but that we're not taught how to make it work.

We're forced to learn other basic life skills. Language. Math. We happily sign up for knitting classes and read cookbooks. But how many of us willingly study relationships?

"You know, Karl and I have had several counselling sessions over the years," Becki admitted.

"What?"

"Surprised?"

"You and Karl?"

"We're not perfect."

"You always seem so happy."

"It takes a lot of work to be happy."

"Well I'm prepared to work."

"And Tony?"

"I think so."

"So the issue is just trust then…" How much should she share? "You want to know an exercise a therapist had Karl and me do once?"

"Sure."

"We laid a mattress—"

"Do I really want to hear this?"

"No sex."

"Okay."

"We laid a mattress or something on the ground and then we had to take turns falling backwards into each other's arms. Could you do that with Tony?"

"Um." Gina looked up at Becki.

"Do you think he would catch you?"

Chapter 26

Cathy was also thinking about marriage. Specifically, the possibility of marrying the man who had been the love of her life.

She was gloriously happy.

After three hours in the beauty salon, her honey coloured hair was streaked with blonde. Her nails were painted a flirty pink. This was to please Garry. He had never gone in for the vamp look, she remembered.

"You look terrific," said Yvette, the senior stylist, at the marble counter when Cathy was paying the bill.

"I was thinking the same thing," said Tiffany, the young manicurist. "That's a killer dress, by the way."

"Have you lost weight?" said Yvette. She had micrometer eyes.

All the women in the salon watched each other's weight as well as their own.

Cathy smiled.

"A little." She let them think it was that.

But this part was true. She felt twenty years younger. It wasn't just the new Adrienne Vittadini dress. It was love.

*It could work this time. It **will** work this time.* Cathy was determined.

Now, was different. Now, there was no wife for him to feel guilty about.

Louisa was dead.

No other woman stood in the way of what Cathy wanted.

It wasn't money. No, she had enough money for both of them. What Cathy wanted was the man she had lost to prison, years ago. The man who, even before that time, she never totally had to herself.

Cathy left the salon, swinging her Kate Spade handbag, and headed down Cumberland.

All other things could be managed. Who cared about the law and a few old business acquaintances? Garry was obsessed with things that didn't matter.

She would have to convince him of that.

They could fly to another city and start over. Maybe someplace warm, like Arizona. Settle in Tucson. Not Phoenix, where their old set had homes. Maybe even Sedona…somewhere tucked away from crowds.

And she would have Garry all to herself. Finally.

As she turned the corner, she thought back to her younger days. Had she really wanted Garry to leave his wife, way back then?

To be honest, she didn't have an answer. The younger Cathy had wanted the thrill of an affair. She had bathed in the giddy feeling of being loved extravagantly, and being considered worth the risk.

Had their affair continued to progress over months and even years, what would have happened? Would Garry have wanted to marry her? Would she have pressed her husband for a divorce, in that eventuality?

Well, the divorce came anyway, but later, and not prompted by her.

By that time, Garry was lost to her, behind bars.

No need to think about that now. Instead, she could think about the days to come.

She walked determinedly down the busy city sidewalk, with a definite spring to her step.

Her feet seemed to stop automatically in front of Bella Sposa.

"Sorry," muttered a younger woman, who bumped into her.

Cathy hardly noticed. She was remembering something Anna had said.

This was the store where Gina had bought her wedding dress.

In the window was a collection of stunning white confections that looked as if they had walked off the pages of *Vogue Magazine*. This was the stuff of dreams.

Nothing suitable for an older bride, of course.

Cathy smiled to herself. She would look ridiculous in these sweeping bridal dresses that had the look of so many Disney Princess gowns.

But the shop would have other, more suitable designer ensembles, she knew. Perhaps even in the Mother of the Bride department.

She hesitated. It was too soon. Garry hadn't mentioned anything about the future, except for getting his money back. She didn't want to jinx anything.

But the impulse was too great. She ran up the steps to the entrance.

What happened next was probably the most blissful hour of Cathy's life.

They treated her like a queen, of course. Gown after gown came out, each dripping with glamour and sophistication.

"So many times, we get these young girls," said the well-groomed sales associate, shaking her head. "Prom dresses!"

"Pardon?"

"They all want poufy prom dresses for their wedding."

Cathy smiled.

"Either that, or something so sexy it's indecent."

"It could be those reality shows," said Cathy.

"They simply have no idea how to dress," said the manager, who brought her a thin flute of champagne.

"A summer bride is so delightful for us."

"Oh, I don't know if we will be married in summer," Cathy said, hastily. "I'm not sure when he will be able to get away. It may be more of a spur of the moment thing." *No kidding,* she thought ruefully.

The manager tittered. "Sonia meant a woman in the summer of her life. You are too young to be considered in your autumn years."

That made her feel good.

"If your date is indefinite, perhaps you would like to look at our ready-to-wear collection? We have several beautiful and eminently suitable gowns in your size that you could take with you today, if they don't require alterations."

Cathy brightened at that. It would be great to walk out with something now. Then she could be ready for whenever, and not make a big deal about it. She was pretty sure Garry wasn't the type to enjoy a fuss.

They had lots in her size. She pawed through the first ten or so designer gowns, becoming more excited with each minute. All the big names were represented here. Vera Wang, Maggie Sottero, Pnina Tornai...

Bliss!

Finally, she pulled three dresses from the rack.

"Let me start with these."

"Perfect! You can't imagine what a pleasure it is for us to help a woman of your discerning taste," said the first.

Cathy lapped it up.

An hour later, when she had just about settled on a Grace Kelly-style ice blue raw silk sheath, Cathy's cellphone rang. She clicked it on.

"Where are you?" said Garry. "I tried the salon. They said you had left." His voice sounded brusque.

"At a bridal shop downtown," she said, automatically fingering the fabric.

Pause.

"Who's getting married?"

Cathy felt panic. She thought fast. "Gina Monroe from The Weather Network. Remember, I told you I knew her mother. We're on the hospital guild together." She was over-explaining, she knew.

"Stay right where you are. Don't move. I'll come and pick you up. Give me the address."

Cathy remained vaguely puzzled as she clicked off the phone. She was fine with taking taxis, but it was nice to be picked up, of course. Showed that he cared.

Which brought her back to the current dilemma.

Should she take the ice blue sheath? Or the oyster one-shoulder with the shearing that gave her such a nice shape? The ice blue would need to be shortened. She would have to come back for it.

The one-shoulder gown was flattering, but damn, she loved the ice blue.

What the hell. You only get married once for the second time.

"I'll take both," she said happily.

Chapter 27

"Bring me the jewels and nobody will get hurt."

"Joshua?" Gina said into the handset again. TV people could be really weird sometimes. Most especially eccentric and flamboyant film critic Joshua Johnson. That must be what this was— Toronto's second most popular film buff playing some gangster movie prank. "Joshua, what's this about, really?" Today she was super busy at work. No time for jokes.

"Stop calling me Joshua."

"What would you like me to call you?" *Did I really succumb to saying that?*

"Shut up and listen."

Gina yanked the handset from her ear, her face twisted in confusion and anger. Hesitantly, she brought the receiver back.

"Bring the jewels to your wedding. Put them on the far end of the bench on the right side of the church vestibule, going in. Then walk down the aisle and forget all about them."

"Huh?"

"Gina, don't play dumb with me. All your loved ones will be there on Saturday, won't they? You don't want anything to happen to them. Or to you."

Gina felt the hairs bristle on the backs of her arms and a sensation of chill swept over her. This wasn't even slightly funny.

"A very simple transaction and you'll never hear from me again."

"But... How—"

Click.

She took a few deep breaths. A few moments to collect herself. Then she pulled her torso up straight in her chair and called Kristen.

"Kristen, did my last caller give his name?"

"No, he just asked for you directly and I put him through."

"Is there any way to trace his call?"

Kristen paused for a moment on the line. *Not a request she gets frequently.*

"Um. Maybe. I don't know how to do it personally."

"Can you call the cops for me and patch them through?"

"Certainly."

Singapore Noodles is Toronto comfort food, thought Becki. *That's why Gina chose to bring the dish home, plop the brown paper bag down on the counter, and why she's now hastily and distractedly hunting for plates to serve it in.*

"Pasta plates…" Gina mumbled.

Becki dared not interrupt her. Not yet. She already knew something was wrong. Something big. *Shit. Shit. Shit.* The *what* would come later. She helped her friend by tearing open the bag and pulling out the two sets of wooden chopsticks, fused together at the top and enveloped in a translucent paper sheath. Napkins, a huge lidded plastic container of noodles, Chinese Almond Cookies and Fortune Cookies for later.

She pried open the lid of the main entrée. The bolstering scent of curry wafted up. Usually the rice noodles would be fried with shrimp and chicken but Gina had ordered the veggie version just to please. All the regular vegetables like julienne of onion and carrot, bean sprouts, plus scrambled egg and tiny cubes of tofu. Becki arranged the meal buffet-style and went to grab drinks from the fridge.

"Okay, now hit me," she said, once they'd eaten about half the noodles. *Gina must feel a bit better now.*

"I got a call at work today."

Becki didn't mention that Gina must get plenty of calls at work.

"It was a threat."

Becki's chopsticks slipped from mid-air down to her plate. "A threat? Yikes! About what?"

Gina relayed the gist of it.

Since Becki had unconsciously been clenching her abdomen muscles, she took a breath then exhaled with, "Oh my God!" got up, rounded the bar and hugged her friend.

Gina was obviously trembling even though it had to be 25°C in the condo.

The next question was self-evident. "Was this person a man or a woman?"

"Man."

"Um…okay—"

"Or a woman disguising herself as a man," continued Gina. "So easy to do with electronics, Tony says."

"Now we're really getting somewhere," ventured Becki.

Gina pouted but a grin lurked beneath. "I called the cops," she added.

"Of course."

"This is nuts, Becki, my wedding is already crawling with cops."

"You're referring to my dear husband and, well, your own beloved?"

"But a cops and robbers theme was not what I had in mind!"

Gina was finally loosening up. Becki rubbed her back one more time then returned to her chair. Perhaps now it would be safe to delve further. Becki asked, "Do you think jewels refer to the necklace set discovered in the strongbox hidden in Louisa's wall?"

"First thing that crossed my mind. Um, after I realized we weren't talking about a movie featuring James Cagney. Why the hell would someone think I have those jewels anyway?"

Another mouthful of spicy noodles helped Becki think things through out loud. "The person who wants the necklace couldn't find it in Louisa's house, so of course he/she assumes someone else found it first."

"Why assume it was me for heaven's sake? We *do* have a few real suspects in Louisa's murder."

"That's just it. *We* have a few suspects. But do our suspects even know about each other?"

"Who've we got? Lottie the friend, Garry the ex, Sylvia the maid, Douglas the developer…"

"Not the strongest connections. And yet everyone knows about you, Gina. You were in the newspaper article about the murder. You're on The Weather Network. You're also in the paper about your wedding."

"Yes, someone clearly thinks I'm another misbehaving Canadian personality."

"Ha!"

"Okay," Gina said, "so what I don't get is, if someone is looking for the jewels, why in hell would he/she burn down Louisa's place? What's the motivation for that? Seems kinda counterproductive to me."

"I agree. But who says it wasn't just kids having a party in the empty house that started the fire? We haven't got anything on that yet. And, um, maybe because of it, we good guys caught a lucky break. Has to happen once in a while, doesn't it?"

"I suppose."

"If the place hadn't burned down, *we* never would have found the jewels either."

"Are you saying that Louisa was murdered for those jewels but we might never have known that, and on top of that it might all have been for nothing because they would have remained buried in the wall?"

"That's what I'm saying."

"God rest her soul."

"Hear, hear," Becki said. Then with a noise somewhere between a cough and clearing her throat, she added, "Maybe Louisa and you aren't the only ones some bad guy is after."

"What?"

"When you listed our suspects just now, you got me thinking. Do you know that Sylvia was run down by a car in Black Currant Bay?"

"No, that's horrible!"

"I know."

"Is she...dead?"

"Luckily not. But Karl did go the hospital to talk to her and he reported she's real banged up."

"A coincidence that Louisa is murdered and then her cleaning lady is struck by a car?"

"Maybe, but I got the distinct sense that Sylvia was targeted."

"How did you get that feeling?" Gina scrunched up her face.

"I saw it happen."

Gina's jaw dropped.

"I've been playing the scene over and over again in my mind."

"How did it go?"

"This big, dark blue car with a silvery quality—my eye for colour is coming in handy here—appears to veer out of control, crashes into Sylvia, but then manages to straighten itself out and speed away from the scene. Which in and of itself is illegal."

"Did you get the plate number?"

"No, and I'm kicking myself for that. The only clue is a hub cap that was left at the scene. Karl's working on that, but it's going to take a while because there are many models of hub cap out there that fit lots of different cars."

"And you're just telling me this now, Becki?"

"Because it's so close to your wedding day and we've been so busy with other activities and considerations..." Becki's voice tapered to a whisper.

"What's your fortune cookie say?" Gina asked suddenly.

On cue, Becki broke open her crisp wafer, extracted the tiny slip of white paper. She cleared her throat then read, "In prosperity, our friends know us. In adversity we know our friends."

Gina grabbed her hand and squeezed.

"Yours?" Becki asked.

"Don't be afraid to smile, you never know who's falling in love with it!"

"Perfect!" Becki said.

Chapter 28

Gina gazed at the morning paper in disbelief.

"Treasure Found in Wall of Victim's House" read a headline.

Her frantic eyes scanned the article...*New developments in the murder case of Louisa Davidson. Diamond and sapphire necklace found at the scene of the burned out house...*

Gina sat back on the island stool, her mind speeding through scenarios. *The Toronto paper, dammit!* How did a Toronto reporter find out about the necklace in the wall? Who the heck had spilled the beans? One of the cops in bed with the media?

Or was it one of the firemen at the discovery?

One thing was for sure, she was convinced Karl wouldn't have spoken about this. And it sure wasn't Becki or her.

But someone must have leaked it to the Toronto paper, and Karl was going to be furious when he found out.

What should she do?

The phone rang. Gina reached for it automatically.

"Did you see in the paper, about the necklace?" said Anna.

Gina nodded, and then realized her mother couldn't hear that.

"How could they have found out?" Gina blurted out the question in her head.

Silence. *Okay, that sentence was a little ambiguous,* Gina thought. She strove for clarity in the next one. "The papers, I mean. Who could have told them?"

Whoops. She realized her mistake almost instantly.

"So you knew about the necklace, Gina?"

Best to come clean when it's your mom.

"Becki called me about it. Karl wanted my opinion on whether it could be real."

"And?"

"It's real. They sent me a photo. 18 carat gold—I had them check for the mark."

More silence.

"You better phone Becki so she can tell Karl the cat is out of the bag," said Anna.

Now Gina was silent.

"You have to, Gina. It could jeopardize his investigation. He needs to know."

"I know," said Gina, swallowing hard. This wasn't going to go over well. And there was something else that bothered her even more.

She anticipated her mother's next question.

"Are you going to tell Tony?"

"I don't think so," she said.

Karl looked down at the business card in his hand.

The last person he was expecting to see at the station house was Tony Ferrero. *Tony? Three hours away from his beloved Toronto, in this northern Ontario backwater of Black Currant Bay?*

"He says he can't wait long," said Mary, the elderly gal on reception who had once been a ringer for Ann Baxter.

"I'll come out," Karl said, swinging his long legs out from behind the desk.

It had been a hell of a busy day so far. Call out to a car accident on the highway. That had ended badly for one driver.

He'd only just gotten back to his desk, and now this.

His mind was whirling. *Tony wouldn't be here unless it was something about the girls. Something important.*

Tony was standing, not sitting, of course. His curly brown hair was cut shorter than usual, but still, the stance was unmistakable. He stood looking out the front window with his arms crossed on his chest. No slick suit today—he was dressed in a golf shirt and jeans.

His back was rigid, as if poised to move swiftly. Everything about the man spoke of quick, definite movement.

The sound of footsteps brought him around.

"Tony," Karl said. "What brings you up here?"

Tony grasped the hand offered and pumped it firmly.

"Place we can talk privately—maybe outside?"

Karl smiled. That was Tony, all right. No stopping for small talk.

He glanced over at the reception desk. "Mary, I'll be back in ten."

Mary smiled back at him.

Karl held open the door. "Back of the station. We have a picnic table." He led the way around the side of the building, past the neglected morning glories that clung valiantly to the old wooden trellis.

The picnic table was equally neglected. Once, it had been painted a rich green. Some spots of that colour had yet to peel off the grey of the weathered wood.

Karl threw himself down on the far bench. Tony more carefully slipped onto the bench on the other side. Again, Karl smiled to himself.

"What's up?" he said.

"I wanted to talk to you about the phone call."

"What phone call?" Karl could see the other man start.

"About the jewelry. Becki didn't tell you?"

Karl pulled himself straight. "Tell me what?"

An hour later, Tony had started back to the city.

Karl drove along the coast road to home. He was still angry. Thing was, he couldn't figure out who he was angrier *with*. The knobs in the Toronto force who hadn't bothered to pass on news about the phone call threat? It had a direct bearing on his case, dammit!

Or his beloved wife who usually told him everything? She hadn't even mentioned it on the phone last night!

Oh right. They didn't talk last night, because he had been out at the softball game.

At the stop light in the centre of town, he slammed his hand on the wheel. He hated to be taken by surprise by things like this. Especially by people like Tony.

Yeah, he liked the guy, which was a good thing since Gina was marrying him. And yeah, the man had been good at his spook job, no question about that. But it rankled to be out-maneuvered by a non-cop, no matter what his background.

But Tony had a good plan, he reflected. The chance was too good to be missed. Yes, they were both a little nervous about having the girls there. But everything revolved around the church wedding, and it would be kind of hard to make that happen without the bride and the matron of honour.

Which brought him back to the thing that really pissed him off. Why hadn't Becki called him?

Something chirped. Tinny sound, not like a bird. It took him a moment to remember that it was his cellphone, so rarely did he think to use it. He pulled over to the side to look at it. *Six unanswered calls and two texts. Shit*, he thought. *I hate cellphones.*

"Couldn't we at least stay at a nice place in Toronto?" Cathy looked around the dismal motel room with despair. Drab colours of dull burgundy and muted green were repeated everywhere on the floor, window coverings and bedclothes.

The suburbs were nice, she imagined, if you could buy a big house on the lakefront and belong to the yacht club. But being stuck in a chain motel next to a gas station and some fast food joints was no thrill.

"Can't risk it," Garry said. "No one would ever think of looking for me here."

Cathy frowned. That was true. No one she knew would be caught dead in such a place. So why exactly were they here? Who was he afraid of?

Yesterday had been a whirlwind. Garry had shown up at the bridal store with a suitcase already packed for her. All the wrong clothes she had found out later, when she opened the case. She had actually laughed out loud and received a rueful smile in return. Why a man would pack two evening dresses and yet no shoes or pantyhose to go with it. Not to mention, a strapless bra...

And apparently, the bathroom didn't even cross his mind. She always had the basics in her purse—lipstick, mascara, powder—but she would have to stop at a makeup counter for sure.

Obviously he had been greatly distressed and packed in a hurry. Since then, he had been strangely closed-mouth, although delightfully amorous.

They had had room service last night and this morning. And lots of loving in between.

Hard to complain, when the love of your life whisks you off in a modern day chariot. But she worried. Somehow she had to get Garry to talk.

Cathy watched him work at the small desk, pounding the laptop with two fingers.

"This place will be okay for now," he said, not even turning his head. "Oakville has some nice shops downtown. Why don't you take the car? You said you had some essentials to get."

Again, that absentminded voice...talking the words, and yet it's clear he doesn't give a hoot what he's saying. How does he do that?

"Will you come too?" she ventured.

He obviously hadn't heard her. "It won't be long. Just until Saturday. Then we can go wherever you like, as long as it's outside of the country."

Saturday...something was happening Saturday. Oh right—that was Gina's wedding day.

But her mind latched on to another phrase.

Outside of the country? That was cool.

"Are you ordering tickets to somewhere?"

His hands paused over the keyboard. He turned now, and surveyed her face for a moment. He seemed to be drinking her in, like his soul needed sustenance. It was the kind of look every woman dreamed about, and Cathy was no exception. She sat on the bed, with her hands demurely in her lap, and felt the love wash over her. Bliss.

Then his rugged face broke into a smile.

"Not yet. But I can. Where would you like to go?"

Now her mind was on honeymoon spots. Finally, the man of her dreams was going to take her to someplace romantic. They could get married there. Thank God she had already taken the one dress from the bridal store.

Everything else, she could get in downtown Oakville, or abroad.

Abroad! A wedding abroad!

"Rome," she said happily. "I'd like to go to Rome."

Chapter 29

Becki and Gina sat side by side in leather swivel chairs in Douglas Spellman's office located in the rear of the Douglas Spellman Corporation building. The company's main office structure was clean and contemporary and it occupied a generous lot in a well-tended industrial park in the Steeles Avenue West and Keele Street area of North Toronto. Still, Becki smelled skunk.

She'd disliked Spellman from the moment she spotted him slinking around Louisa's property. Furthermore, his attitude when they met at her store had surely not endeared him to her and this afternoon he irritated further as he strutted behind his desk and expounded on his accomplishments.

"Douglas Spellman Corporation is committed to building homes of the highest quality. Over the last ten years, Spellman has built more than 10,000 new homes, working diligently to earn its reputation as one of Canada's top builders of luxury communities."

Nothing wrong with being proud of what you do but pompousness is so unnecessary.

Because he was on a roll and thus giving her plenty of time to observe, she spent a few more moments speculating. *No wedding ring tying him down so I bet he enjoys making a splash with the ladies, who probably go for his vivid blue eyes...and his millions.*

The man's 40 years old or thereabouts, likely too young to have built all this from scratch himself. Daddy had a hand in it, at least financially. Let's see, plenty of degrees on the wall so he's a smart guy, but smarmy in a way that reveals that should he find an easier-than-kosher method to accomplish a goal, he'll jump on it.

"Does that help you at all, Ms. Green?"

Becki nearly leaped out of her seat at being addressed. His whole speech up until now had basically been for Gina's benefit. Another behaviour Becki couldn't stand—the way some people ignore those they consider less relevant. Like female waiters who play up to the male diner when serving a couple.

"Yes, thank you, Mr. Spellman."

In Black Currant Bay she had requested they cut to first names, but here she figured they might as well stick to what he obviously preferred, formal address. This was a pseudo business meeting after all. Her pretext for being here was to verify a few points with regard to the decoration of the sales centre/model home soon to be built in Black Currant Bay.

"As I mentioned on the phone," she'd begun when they first sat down, "I happen to be in Toronto for Gina's wedding," here she'd smiled genuinely at her friend, "and I thought I should take advantage of the opportunity to meet with you one more time and get a direct feel for your company and what you represent."

Now it was time to ease into what she and Gina were really fishing for, having done some initial research online. *Here goes.*

"The Spellman name has been around a long time in Toronto," she prompted.

Douglas opened his mouth and looked dying to jump in here but she embellished. "I'd include it among prominent Toronto families like the Mitchells and the Davenports. If I may be so bold, are you one of *the* Spellmans?"

"Proud of it," he said, smirking. "I'm gratified by the contribution our family made to this city over the years. Thrilled to be continuing in my father's and grandfather's footsteps."

Falling into their unique version of bad cop/good cop, it was Gina's turn to pipe up.

Gina was stunning on TV but in the flesh she could lead a man into confessing just about anything. The poor sop would never for a minute question motive. He would just fall all over himself trying to please.

"My mother is on the edge of that crowd," Gina began. She crossed a lovely bare leg over the other. No *Basic Instinct* shenanigans. Gina was classy. Relaxed. Just offering idle conversation. And a dazzling smile. "You must remember the scandal when Garry Davenport and his wife broke up and he was ultimately sent to jail!"

"The media ate that up, didn't they?" Douglas sat down at his desk and leaned toward Gina conspiratorially.

Obviously not deterred by the earlier mention of Gina's impending nuptials.

"You must have been in a position to hear the inside scoop." Gina was practically whispering.

"Oh yes. Linda Davenport disappearing, rumours of mob interests, missing jewels—" His cerulean eyes flashed. They darted between the two friends.

He pulled back in his chair. "I'm sure you didn't come here to talk about ancient gossip."

Time to kick this pop stand, thought Becki.

"Mr. Spellman," she said, "I appreciate you taking time out of your busy day to speak about your company and its ambitions in Black Currant Bay. I'm sure you'll be pleased with what Beautiful Things comes up with for the model."

"I'm sure I will." He rose, officially signalling the end of the meeting. "Thanks for coming in."

Surprisingly, he didn't offer his hand and neither did they as he led them to the doorway, where Gina did blast him with one more grin. It seemed to leave him flustered. He half-waved as the friends shuffled through the doorframe and then he shut his heavy office door behind them.

Still, Becki and Gina didn't say a thing to each other until they were safely back in Gina's car. In these days of security cameras everywhere, the walls have eyes and ears.

"What do you think?" Becki asked as they pulled out of the parking lot.

"He didn't look at all nervous when we walked in, did he? Not like someone who had just threatened me, my family and my friends."

"Could he be that good an actor?"

"In my opinion, business execs are all sales guys and all very good actors. The more successful the exec, the bigger the camouflaged load of shit. The same for politicians."

"How cynical you are!" Becki teased.

"Just being realistic."

"I, on the other hand, like to think there are plenty of exceptions. Execs and salespeople who are genuinely excited about their product. And politicians who really want to make a difference."

"Do we see Douglas Spellman as an exception?"

Together they shouted, "No!"

"He knows the story of the Davenports," stated Gina.

"More intimately than most," Becki agreed.

"Could he have made the connection to Louisa while researching the development in Black Currant Bay? We've got to remember that this all started when someone sent Louisa flying down her basement stairs."

"Maybe Douglas Spellman met with Louisa to try and convince her to sell her house and recognized her as Linda Davenport at that time. What happened next? Did she not only refuse to sell her home but…but also to be blackmailed into handing over valuables from her former life?"

"In the end, Spellman would know, wouldn't he, that exposing Louisa would in fact get him no closer to her loot? If anything, her hidden assets would fall into the government's hands because of the Davenport's earlier bankruptcy. Is it possible, then, that to satisfy a twofold objective—develop her land and grab some jewels while he's at it—Spellman killed her?"

"Her property in Black Currant Bay would thus become available to him and be easily searchable. Here's something else," Becki said, turning toward Gina who was concentrating on the road as they approached a busy intersection. "Why would Douglas Spellman himself spend the amount of time he did in Black Currant Bay? Speaking strictly in terms of business, you'd think an underling would be sent all the way up north from Toronto to work the details of the project. Since when does an owner himself do that kind of legwork solitarily?"

"I didn't recognize him as the voice on the phone."

"You wouldn't."

Gina's eyes continued to stare confidently through the windshield at the traffic ahead but her sparkling white teeth worried her bottom lip.

"You don't think whoever called me would really hurt me and my family, do you? I mean, this can't be serious. He's just trying to scare me into giving up the jewels, which he thinks I have. Right?"

"I wonder if that's how Louisa looked at it." Becki hated the way her answer echoed in the interior of Gina's Camaro.

She searched quickly for another topic of conversation. Something to lighten the mood.

"Can you believe your rehearsal supper is in just two days?" she said.

"It's going fast now, isn't it?" Gina replied.

"You bet. By Saturday night you, my friend, will be a married woman."

Chapter 30

When Gina got home, a surprise awaited her.

Tony. He was standing in the kitchen, leaning against the granite counter, reading a newspaper. As always, her heart rate sped up to a ridiculous number when she saw him.

"What are you doing here?" she blurted.

Crap. That was the wrong thing to say. It even *sounded* like she was guilty of something. She placed her purse on the bench beside the door, and deliberately avoided his eyes.

"Waiting for you. Obviously." His voice sounded grimly amused.

Gina paused. "That didn't come out right. I mean, it's good that you're here. I just wasn't expecting you tonight."

Tony pushed up from the counter. "I thought we better talk. It's becoming pretty clear that you and Becki aren't leaving this murder alone. So I've decided to help."

Gina hesitated. Damn Tony! He put things in such a way that she had to admit to it, or at least address it.

"How do you know we aren't leaving it alone?"

"That visit to Spellman today, for one." He crossed his arms in a deliberate power move.

Her jaw dropped. "How did you know about that?"

"Gina, are you nuts? That guy is dangerous. He's a crooked developer, and you know the links they have. What did you think you were doing, forcing him into a corner with questions? If he's the killer, you've just alerted him that you're a threat."

Gina stared at him. He was right, of course. What they had done today was foolhardy. She had worried about it all the way home in the car.

"How did you know?" she repeated, unable to think of anything else to say.

"How do you think?" Tony said. "It's my business to know things."

"Not any more, it isn't supposed to be," Gina shot back.

There was an awkward silence.

Finally, Tony spoke. "Don't be naïve. A tiger doesn't lose his hunting ability just because he's in a cage."

Cage. That word hit Gina like a strike to the face.

"You feel like you're in a cage?"

Tony shook his head. "Don't twist this into something it isn't. I didn't mean getting married. I meant, I've been trained to observe and investigate. Those skills don't go away just because I've chosen a new line of work."

But Gina was still back on the word *cage.* It was the one thing—the only thing—that could really shake her up. The fear that Tony would feel trapped after they were married.

"It's clear to me that you two aren't going to let this alone, Gina. God help me, I wish you would. It's also clear I can't stop you. So don't shut me out. Let me help. Tell me what you and Becki are planning to do, and I'll do my best to help you do it safely." Tony came around the island and leaned back on it.

Gina felt relief wash over her. "Really?"

It seemed incredible. Garry actually wanted to go to Gina Monroe's wedding on Saturday! Cathy could hardly believe it. Her face must have reflected this mild astonishment.

"What's wrong? Don't you want to take me as your guest?" Garry frowned at her.

"It's not that," Cathy rushed to reassure him. "I just never thought you'd want to go. It never occurred to me to ask you."

Indeed, it hadn't. She had completely forgotten about Gina's wedding.

"Is she expecting you to go?" Garry's voice brought her back to the shabby motel room. He was sitting in the hotel room's only easy chair, leaning back with his legs crossed in that masculine way, with one ankle resting on the other knee.

"Well that's the embarrassing thing." Cathy giggled. "Certainly, I had intended to go. But since you whisked me off here, I hadn't even thought about it. Probably, I would have forgotten completely if you hadn't mentioned it."

That would have been embarrassing, all right. Not showing up because you forgot? What an insult to the family! Especially since the entire women's committee at the hospital, and heck, the whole of Toronto society was going to be there.

Her mind fast-forwarded to what she could wear. The oyster one-shoulder was going to be her bridal gown. She had intended to wear something knee-length to Gina's wedding, but that dress wasn't in her suitcase.

She simply had to get back to Bella Sposa to pick up that ice blue silk.

"So she's expecting you. Will she be expecting you to bring a guest?"

Cathy hesitated. "I can't remember how I rsvp'd. But I'm sure it wouldn't be a problem. I could email her to make sure."

Wait a minute. Could she? Did she even have Gina's email? Oh, but surely it would be online, listed with The Weather Network. If not, she could phone her. Cathy did have Gina's phone number.

"Probably better you don't do that. I wouldn't ask them to do anything now that might upset plans. They'll be busy. If there isn't enough room for me at dinner, I could just go to the wedding."

"I'm sure they would insist you stay for the reception." Cathy was confident about that. Her type of people always acted with courtesy in situations like this. Gina and her mother had class.

Cathy tended to be preoccupied with clothes and jewelry a lot, it was true. But she was no dummy. Garry had rushed her out of the city and seemed to want to lay low. This was a sudden reversal. It stuck out a mile to her that something was afoot.

"But Garry, why do you want to go?"

Garry pushed himself up from the chair. He came over to sit beside her on the bed. Then he picked up her right hand in his and covered it with his left.

"Let me tell you."

Lottie had her dress all chosen. It was turquoise, a shade she just loved, but could rarely find. Her shoes weren't perfect, alas. Beige didn't clash with turquoise, but it was such a plain colour. The shoes just didn't match the beauty of the dress.

One couldn't have everything, she chided herself. She simply had to save every penny she could for the trip to Cornwall. And besides, she had already spent a small fortune for the bus fare to Toronto.

Thing was, nobody knew she was coming this weekend, so there was nobody she could hitch a ride with. It was going to be a surprise!

Lottie preened at how clever she had been. Weddings weren't actually private. You needed an invitation to a reception, because they provided food there. The caterers had to plan for a certain number of people. But anybody could go to a church.

And Lottie was pretty certain that when they saw her at the church, they would of course invite her to the reception. After all, Louisa had received an invitation. And Louisa's place would be empty.

For a moment, she felt a pang. It didn't last long. Yes, it was lonely without Louisa, but there was no sense crying over spilt milk, as her dear mom used to say.

Next, she thought about a wedding gift. Was it necessary? Surely the shower gift was enough?

One wanted to do the right thing, of course. But money was such a problem.

Then she had it! She could say that, in the rush to catch the bus, she forgot the gift at home. Everybody would believe it. Some people considered her scattered, she knew. It actually amused her.

If they could only know what was going on in her mind, and what she was capable of.

Chapter 31

Gina caught herself exhibiting her trademark toothy grin because she had her condo all to herself. However, her pleasure in this fact should not be misinterpreted. In no way was she tired of Becki's company. Hanging out with her these last few days was a dream come true. To have such a confidant ready and willing to lend support and just have fun with her! Priceless!

But clearly it was time to indulge in private time with that handsome, charming rake that she would marry in *three days*.

Tony had invited her out for a candlelit, patio supper. Afterwards they'd strolled the lamp-lit sidewalks in her neighbourhood for over an hour. Because it was one of those balmy June evenings when you never want to go inside, she'd managed to cajole Tony into investigating yet another block further away from her condo.

There was just one thing that could entice her to willingly turn for home.

Tony finally clued in.

"So what are the rules?"

"Rules?" Sometimes it's best to play innocent.

"Well…we established weeks ago that I'm not allowed to see your dress. 'Until the day of' you said. Is there anything else restricted? Perhaps something else I'm not allowed to see?"

They were walking hand in hand. His palm pressed hot against hers.

"What else is there that you haven't seen, Tony?" She twisted her shoulders to peer at him in the dim light.

"We haven't been together in a while."

"Yes but there are no surprises in that department."

"On the contrary." He leaned in and kissed her passionately. "You're full of spectacular surprises."

What a delicious kiss!

Almost as intoxicating as their very first kiss, which admittedly had been a doozy since they had originally thought...well, that was the past. *This man wants you and always will. Moreover, you want him. Love him. Adore him!*

Neither of them wanted to appear to be hurrying back to the condo.

Back in her bedroom, Gina was torn between not wanting to separate from Tony and wanting to refresh herself.

Perhaps she chose wrong.

When they were no longer touching and the en-suite door stood closed between them, their earlier conversation snuck like an opportunistic thief back into her head.

Cage.

Tony had said he'd give up the Canadian Security Intelligence Service. Period. In fact, he promised he'd no longer be an Intelligence Officer by the time they said their wedding vows.

Fair or not, she needed this because Intelligence Officers had to "agree to relocate anywhere in Canada and/or abroad, depending on the requirements of the Service, throughout your career." A declaration right there on the CSIS website.

She was not leaving Canada. She was not raising kids all over the country.

Kids needed a father who was present and most of all *alive*.

Tony claimed he was prepared for as many kids as she wanted. And a dog.

But he's a spy and spies lie, right?

She loved him.

Did she trust him?

It was ironic that he submitted to an extensive investigation involving verification of all personal and financial information, polygraph testing and fingerprinting for his job.

Trust.

Her thoughts spun until they landed on her conversation with Becki.

Why not do that experiment in trust that Becki talked about?

Tonight.

If I'm playful, he'll never know it's a test and this is as much for his benefit as for me.

She opened the bathroom door.

"Wow," whispered Tony.

While they kissed and clung to each other, time seemed suspended. When Gina was finally able to take a breath she dared to suggest, "Let's do an experiment."

"I'm game," Tony said, his voice hoarse.

"Stand up."

"Right here?"

"Yes, here on the bed."

"Okay."

He climbed up on his knees and then to his feet. The mattress sagged beneath his weight. He wobbled as if on a trampoline. A gorgeous statue of a man on a trampoline...

Gina almost forgot what she was doing. "Um, okay, step back toward the head of the bed and I'm going to..." She said this as she was rising to her own feet. "...turn around and fall backwards—"

"What?"

"And you catch me."

"What kind of new-fangled...?"

Gina relented and explained, "It's an exercise in trust."

Tony's open expression closed.

Uh-oh.

"You've got to be kidding," he said.

Chapter 32

Can you marry someone you don't trust?

More to the point—should you marry someone who doesn't trust *you*?

Tony was in a filthy mood. Last night had not gone according to plan.

He'd gone through the crazy trust exercise with Gina. He'd caught her competently in his arms, when she fell backwards. He didn't even lose his balance on the wobbly mattress. Such was his physical prowess.

But his amour prop had suffered.

Gina didn't trust him.

How in hell could he get around that?

After the fated fall, the telephone had rung. It was Gina's mother, and Gina felt obligated to take the call.

Whether it was the mother on the phone, or the trust issue hanging in the air, Tony couldn't determine. But he sure wasn't 'in the mood' anymore. In fact, it seemed almost indecent waiting around in a partial state of undress.

He stood up and gathered his clothes and shoes. He left the bedroom and strode to the kitchen. There, he wrote a note, a sincere, heartfelt note, which he left on the granite counter. In it, he said that he loved her with all his heart, and trusted her, and hoped she did the same. He ended it with 'Love Tony.' Then he left the condo.

That had been twelve hours ago. Night had come and gone. Coffee had been consumed along with a stale breakfast muffin. He wanted to text Gina now. Badly. But he couldn't think of a thing to say.

Meanwhile, Gina was puzzling over something else.

She woke up haunted by the thought of jewelry. Not her gorgeous engagement ring, which had cost the earth. Even so, she couldn't resist looking down at it now. A full carat solitaire, with a ring of diamonds circling it like a crown. Yes, she loved bling, probably more than a sensible person should.

But that wasn't what bothered her now.

Jewelry was something Gina knew about, just as she knew about fashion. What's more, she knew about the women who *had* real jewelry…how they behaved. What they thought. How they felt about it.

So there was one question that still haunted her. Yes, they had found Louisa's sapphire and diamond necklace. *Where was all the other stuff?*

Gina knew that to have a necklace like that was a sign. One didn't have just a single spectacular necklace. There would a score of other gifts leading up to that particular piece.

The women in that privileged circle had piles of expensive jewellery. She'd even heard them talk about 'beginner rings' that would eventually be upgraded, and 'serious gold bracelets' received from the in-laws. The accumulation of jewelry went far beyond the engagement and wedding ring, and the first set of diamond earrings. These women were billboards for their husbands' success.

It didn't just come from old money. The nouveau riche were even more anxious to show off their monetary achievements. Sometimes those wives would show up with a new cocktail ring every year. Sometimes, every gala.

So Louisa would have had a drawer full of 'serious jewelry.' And yes, she might have sold a few pieces to keep herself. But why keep that one? Surely, it would have gone for the most money.

Gina looked down at her hand. Light flashed from the expertly cut solitaire. You had emotional ties with jewelry. Already this diamond had become a part of her. She couldn't imagine ever separating from it.

That made her think about what she would have done in Louisa's place, if she needed money. And that was easy. She would have sold the splashy stuff that wasn't worn often, but that would go for big bucks. That necklace would have been the first to go. Maybe, she would have sold it off to be broken apart, or perhaps she would have peddled each stone individually, over time.

And she would have easily parted with the items that were exclusively gold. Gina didn't have the same attachment to plain gold. Most women didn't. Earrings. Bracelets. It was easy to sell gold by the ounce. They just melted it down.

Gemstones were different. They were unique. You got attached to them in a different way.

The one thing she never would have done was sold off the smaller stuff, the diamond and gemstone earrings and rings, and kept that enormous necklace.

Why? You couldn't wear a necklace like that except at formal events. You also certainly couldn't afford to insure it, if you were short of cash.

Louisa was living a different sort of life in Black Currant Bay. She kept a low profile. She didn't wear ostentatious clothes and jewelry. She didn't go to black tie events.

But Louisa hadn't sold the necklace. That pointed to one thing. Obviously she hadn't needed to. And if she didn't sell the necklace, Gina was willing to bet she hadn't sold all of her smaller, less valuable gemstone jewelry.

Which begged the question, 'where was it *now?*'

Becki had boarded a similar train of thought.

She was staying at Anna's home now. Happily, Anna believed in leisurely mornings. Neither Anna nor Gord were up yet. This gave Becki time to herself, as she was used to rising early with Karl.

Becki had dressed and gone into the cheerful kitchen. She busied herself with the coffeemaker. It would be a nice thing for Anna and Gord to wake up to coffee and a full breakfast.

Becki was thoughtful like that. For instance, she had remembered to bring her own small blue topaz pendant on a gold chain so Gina would have 'something old, something new, something borrowed, something blue' to wear at her wedding. Of course, Gina might already have chosen to borrow 'something old' from her mother. That's why Becki had also brought a lacy blue handkerchief for Gina, in case the necklace wasn't needed.

Necklace. That word kept haunting her.

Becki was a clever, practical woman. Her thoughts were similarly astute.

The necklace. Why had Louisa kept the necklace?

To Becki, that meant one thing. She didn't need the money.

It came to her in such a flash. Yes, they'd missed a step, she and Gina. And Karl too, if she was being honest.

Louisa had been married to a man who ran an entertainment empire. Yes, he had done very well for many years, *but he had obviously come from money.* Becki didn't know how wealthy the original family was, but she knew how these things worked. You had to have capital to start with. Garry Davenport had seed money to build an entertainment empire over fifteen to twenty years. He knew all the right people too. That signalled old money and family connections.

The coffee maker sputtered and dripped in its own language. The aroma was delectable. Becki reached into the cupboard for a mug.

Her thoughts carried back to Louisa. She and Gina had assumed Louisa had made what is euphemistically referred to as a 'good marriage'.

Fair enough.

But Becki knew a lot about people. Most folk mixed with other people in their own circles. Their own money classes. The rich were even more likely to do so.

They sent their kids to private schools so they would only meet kids who were also from rich families. They joined exclusive clubs for the same reason.

She and Gina and Karl—*let's face it, everyone*—had assumed Louisa would need cash to disappear. Why? Why had they thought that?

Surely it made more sense that she had money in her own right. What if she came from a similar well-off family, and had inherited money from her own side? Maybe not millions, but enough to live on?

That was more logical. And that would explain why she hadn't sold the killer necklace.

It would also lead one to wonder—did she have other jewelry they just hadn't found?

That was an intriguing idea. Becki resisted the temptation to focus on that, because she was abruptly aware of a new thought.

All of their investigation so far had been centered on who stood to gain from Louisa's death. Who might have inherited her house, and her savings. Or the necklace.

They had also explored the possibility of Louisa having some knowledge that was dangerous to the mob.

But they'd forgotten one thing.

No one, as far as she knew, had investigated Louisa's original family to see if she stood to inherit money from someone there.

Had Louisa been in line for inheriting something big? Was someone eliminating the competition? And did that 'someone' find out where Louisa—formerly Linda—now lived?

Becki put down the coffee mug. She picked up the phone on the counter and dialed Karl. It was after 11:00, and while Anna's household might be enjoying a leisurely morning, she knew Karl would already be at work. He answered on the second ring.

"Karl, did you ever investigate Louisa's background?"

Pause. Then a weary sigh. "What are you doing now, Becki? I thought you were concentrating on wedding plans, and not the murder."

"The wedding made me think about family connections. Garry Davenport came from money. I'm betting Louisa did too. She probably had money of her own which she was living on."

"So?"

"So, that's why she didn't sell the necklace. She didn't need to."

"Okay. So?"

"So. Louisa's family. She was in late middle-age. That would put the older generation in their late 70s or 80s." *Maybe even 90s.*

"Yeah?" Karl was a patient man. Becki had always been grateful for that.

"What if Louisa was in line to inherit something big?" she said.

Silence on the other end. Then a curse.

"I'm on it."

Becki hung up the phone with a smile on her face.

Chapter 33

Gina had an Oprah-*esque* moment. She was playing amateur sleuth with regard to Louisa's death to distract herself from wedding jitters and it had been working. Unfortunately, right now the only thing she could think of, the only thing she wanted, was to hear from Tony. She pressed both her hands against her stomach, which hurt with her yearning for an in-person greeting. A how're-you-doing phone call. A text. Anything.

When the phone rang, she grabbed it up. "Tony?"

"Sorry, it's just me," Becki said.

"Never say *just* you," Gina replied. Hurting her friend by letting her disappointment show would not do.

"Is he out buying chocolate croissants for a late breakfast?"

I wish. "No, he left last night." Had she kept bitterness and confusion out of her voice?

"You do know that it's only the night right before the wedding that the groom traditionally has to stay away."

She's just teasing. She doesn't realize how bad things are. "Yes I know, but men don't catch the finer points," she said, keeping it light herself. This was just between Tony and her now.

"So what's up today?" Becki asked. "Can I help you with anything?"

"You're a sweetheart for asking but no. As you know, I planned everything months and months in advance. Mostly so these last couple of days before the wedding would be stress free. All I can think of that's left to do is pick up your dress at Bella Sposa tomorrow."

"You don't want me to do that instead? After all, it is my dress. And you're the bride and shouldn't have to do anything more."

"The bride needs to keep herself a little bit busy. Besides, you're keeping my mother out of my hair. I love her to bits but I do need some time alone."

"Not alone-alone."

Becki still assumed she'd be spending the day with Tony. Gina wasn't so sure.

"Yeah, and then at the rehearsal tomorrow we'll all get together and it'll be one great big party."

"Not like the actual wedding."

"Not that spectacular." A girl could still hope.

"Okay Gina, just tell me to shut up if you don't want to hear this right now but I had an idea this morning about the jewelry."

No need to ask 'What jewelry?' "Me too!"

"Louisa had more than just the necklace and earrings they found, didn't she? She must have."

"I agree."

"The person who threatened you talked about jewels, plural, and we assumed he meant the sapphires and diamonds in that one necklace set, but Louisa probably had a treasure trove of jewels."

"What we would consider a fortune."

"It's starting to make sense now that someone is after you about jewels," Becki said. "Someone knew or figured, just like we did, that Louisa had more than one set, even if only the one necklace set was reported found. That person is asking the same question I'm asking myself. Where the hell is the rest?"

"Stolen."

"By who?"

"And how?"

"If Louisa kept her jewels in her safe?"

"Some of it must have been elsewhere at the time of the robbery."

"And murder."

"Louisa must have tucked some hastily in a drawer. Maybe she liked to admire her jewelry pieces like she did her gowns. Maybe she couldn't be bothered putting them away every single time. Maybe she got careless living in sweet little Black Currant Bay. And maybe some of our suspects caught a glimpse of them."

"Not too hard to imagine Sylvia, her cleaning lady, seeing them if Louisa got careless."

"Her main friend, Lottie, too." Gina thought a bit then continued, "We know Douglas Spellman heard rumours about missing jewels, plural, and Louisa's ex would know for sure that she owned a whole collection. Probably gave her most of the pieces himself."

"And the mob?"

"The mob makes it their business to know."

"So precious jewelry is apparently at large. And someone thinks that when we found the body, we searched the house before calling the police and nicked some shiny baubles for ourselves."

"Yeah right. Couldn't be one of Canada's brightest."

"Not so worried about his intellectual profile."

Sylvia almost cried when she zipped up her last suitcase. She'd always wanted to leave Black Currant Bay behind but this was not at all how she pictured it.

In her dreams, she would label only the very best pieces of the furniture and accessories she owned and leave them for a high-end moving company to carefully pack and ship to her new condo in Toronto. She herself would prance out the door in her very best outfit with a small, elegant case of only the choicest garments, jump into her new MINI Cooper S Convertible and zip south to her new place, which would be splendidly decorated and awaiting her arrival.

All the rest she'd leave behind.

The contrast with reality was startling.

She had no new condo to go to. In fact she didn't know where she'd end up exactly. She only knew she had to get out of town.

It was best not to make any arrangements about where she'd stay from her home phone, not even her cell. Phone calls can be traced. Who knew what resources her assailant had at his disposal? For heaven's sake, he had rumoured connections with the mob. *What was I thinking?*

She'd withdrawn everything she had left in her back account. Best to pay cash at an anonymous hotel when she got to TO. *The Greater Toronto Area has roughly six million people in it. Easy enough to disappear.* She'd have to start all over from scratch. She supposed it could be done.

It killed her to have to admit that she was not a big league player.

And she had sat down across the game table from the wrong person.

She stuffed her two ragtag pieces of luggage into the trunk of her MINI Cooper S Convertible. She looked back at her apartment and suddenly felt like it had been a safe haven, a pleasant enough spot after all.

Now she sat awkwardly behind the wheel. Which foot should she use? The heavy right one? Or should she somehow swing her right leg into the passenger space and press on the accelerator and brake with her left?

The more she thought about her situation, the more scared and angry she got. Boiling over with resentment. She would clobber the steering wheel but she was afraid of cracking the only possession she was taking with her that hinted at who she really was and what she was really worth.

She pondered the possibility of testifying to the police truthfully. Telling them what she blackmailed Garry with. That he knew where his ex-wife lived. That she had seen him at the house.

No. That would be a mistake. It would only make things worse.

She pressed the accelerator, too hard of course, and the car jerked backwards, then swung out onto the road and headed to the highway.

In the southbound lane, it was pedal to the metal all the way.

Chapter 34

While waiting at Bella Sposa, Cathy sat in a white leather tub chair, deep in thought. So Garry had arranged to pick up a parcel at the wedding. That didn't seem like a problem, although it was a little odd. He didn't want to tell her more, because it might jeopardize her safety. Cathy smiled. This sounded a lot like a television series, where the hero thinks he's protecting the heroine by limiting her knowledge.

She didn't care. It was almost sweet, in an old-fashioned way. The main thing was, they were going to the wedding, where Garry would pick up a parcel that was important to him. After that, they would go abroad.

Briefly, her mind skipped over the strangeness of collecting something at a wedding. The church was a public place, and a lot of people would be milling around. That was probably it. So the package could be from the mob, and Garry didn't want to meet them in private, for obvious reasons. Safer in a crowd.

"Here it is." Ilonka, the middle-aged sales clerk at Bella Sposa held up the ice blue sheath that had been expertly shortened. "Will you try it on?

Cathy shook her caramel head. "I'm sure it's good. And my fiancé is waiting in the car."

"Perhaps, just to be sure?" The clerk had a voice like honey. "It won't take long. I would hate for something to be wrong."

Cathy hesitated just a second. "Okay." It was too much to resist. She followed the dress into the change room.

Two minutes later, she was modelling the thing in front of a full length, three-way mirror.

"That is truly gorgeous on you!" Ilonka clapped her hands together.

Cathy smiled with delight. It was a perfect fit, nicely sliding over her breasts, skimming her hips, and the hem came just below her knees. Sexy, but appropriate for her age. Luckily, her legs were still good.

"Cathy?"

She whipped her head around.

"Gina! What a nice surprise."

Gina Monroe was always a fashion plate, but today she was dressed in head to toe, skin-clinging Prada. A vision in magenta. Cathy wanted to groan. *Oh to be young and willowy again.*

"Is that the dress you'll be wearing to the wedding? It's stunning," said Gina.

Cathy beamed. "I kind of broke the bank."

"Well, it was worth it," Gina said kindly. "That colour is beautiful with your hair. You look fabulous."

Cathy's heart soared with happiness. She spun in the mirror like a young girl. "Are you here to pick up your wedding dress?"

Gina shook her head. "I've had it for ages. Couldn't resist trying it on every week at home. No, I'm picking up my matron of honour's dress."

"Oh!" said Cathy, feeling impetuous. "Speaking of the wedding, would you mind if I brought a date to the reception?"

Gina smiled. "Of course not. We expected you to."

Cathy breathed with relief. That had been easy! So much better to let everyone know things ahead of time, rather than surprise everyone. Garry didn't understand about things like that.

Another pleasant wave of excitement washed over her. She had a sudden idea.

"Are you leaving now?" said Cathy. "Because he's right outside in the car, waiting for me. I could introduce you."

"Sure," said Gina, without hesitating. "I'll just be in the front, waiting."

"I'll change and be right out."

Cathy hurried through the motions. She stepped out from the changing room and handed the blue silk dress to Ilonka. Within seconds, the dress was placed onto a padded hanger and fitted into a garment bag, ready to go.

Cathy folded the dress bag over her arm and made her thanks. She hurried to the front of the store, where Gina stood. She also had a bag over her arm, and was gazing at a glittering display of shoes. Silk pumps and sandals had been died to jewel colours to match the bridesmaid dresses.

"Lovely things," said Gina. "But I'm not crazy about having everything matchy matchy."

Cathy nodded her agreement. "I can't wear those. Silk doesn't give like leather."

They left the store, both smiling.

It was a beautiful, sunny day in Toronto, the sort of day that made you glad you lived in Southern Ontario. The sky was vivid blue, a colour that you seldom saw in places like England or Vancouver. *Would she miss it,* Cathy wondered? *Surely Rome would have blue skies. Wasn't it inland?*

Cathy led the way to the parking lot. "Follow me," she said. "He's just around the back."

Bella Sposa fronted on a main street, with an alley out the back. Along the back of the building were several parking spots for employees and select customers who had been told they could park there, without paying. This meant something in Toronto, where parking easily topped twelve dollars an hour.

The pavement was rough and breaking up in parts. Someone had tried to fill in the gaps with pea gravel. Hell on heels, and Cathy could see that Gina was having a hard time coping. It was tricky, sort of like walking on ancient uneven paving stones. *Better get used to it*, Cathy thought to herself. Italy would be just like this, and damned if she was going to wear pedestrian running shoes in the land of high fashion.

It was easy to find him. There was no one else in the back lot, and no other car as expensive as this one.

"Not far. He's just over here." Cathy pointed to a dark blue car parked a few spots away.

She quickened her pace. A big smile split her face. She was just so excited and proud to be able to show her man to someone.

Garry opened the driver's door. He stepped out and removed his sunglasses.

His body made a huge, very masculine silhouette against the sun. From this angle, with the sun behind him, you couldn't tell whether he was young or old. Cathy felt a faint stirring, the kind that had been dormant for years, but that had become more common in the last several days.

Damn, she loved this man. Nothing was going to separate them now.

She heard Gina gasp beside her. The dress bag dropped to the ground.

Cathy's head turned to her.

Gina was staring at Garry's Audi. Her eyes were like saucers.

"But that's the car," she said.

"What car?"

"The dark blue car with a silvery quality and a missing hubcap." Gina's voice was thin and strained.

"Gina, what are you talking about?"

"The one Becki described. The one involved in the hit and run."

"What hit and run?" Cathy was bewildered.

"In Black Currant Bay." Gina raised her arm like a zombie and pointed. "It's even got a dent in front where it hit the body."

For a moment everyone froze. Then Garry shot across the distance between them and put his big hand over Gina's mouth. He wrapped his other arm around her body to prevent her struggling.

"Get the back door open," he said to Cathy.

Cathy hesitated. *What was Garry doing?*

"I'm not going to hurt her. We just need to talk," said Garry.

Now she acted. Cathy ran to the back door and swung it open. Garry manhandled Gina into the car, and then got in himself.

"You drive," he said to Cathy. "Keys are in the ignition."

Cathy pushed the back door shut. She fit herself into the front seat and threw her purse and the bag containing her blue silk dress on the passenger seat. Then she checked for child locks. There! She pressed the button so the car doors couldn't be opened from the back seat.

"Smart thinking, sweetheart," Garry said. "Now drive us to the motel."

Cathy started the car and drove steadily out of the parking lot, into the back alley. Her mind was in a maelstrom. It was crazy, insane. But for some reason, Gina was a threat to Garry. And her instinct would always be to protect Garry.

Neither of them gave a thought to Gina's purse or the garment bag which lay forgotten on the broken pavement.

Chapter 35

It was a minute or two past 7:15 p.m. and Anna and Gord's house seemed momentarily hush to Becki except for the ticking of the old-fashioned alarm clock on the guest bedroom night table. But at 7:30 Gina was due to burst in through the front door of the house and lead them all merrily to the church for the rehearsal.

Becki had propped a pink and white quilted pillow against the head of the intricate wrought iron bed she'd been using while staying here. She leaned back comfortably against it and lay down her book to soak in the cozy charm because tonight would be her last night in this lovely room.

Becki figured that Gina had inherited her fashion sense from her mother's obvious décor savvy.

Anna had travelled all over the world with her husband, and had brought back items that she fell in love with to decorate their home. What made her purchases different from those of typical tourists is that she had a gifted eye.

She chose pieces that she could incorporate into her decorating scheme, where they would neither clash nor take over the overall design.

The perfect example lay right here on the floor. The Persian rug—with its jewelled tones of fuchsia and sapphire and of course the graphic strength of black and white—was probably sent home from Iran.

On the wall across from the bed, the framed painting with subtle washes of pastel and bold strokes of India ink that depicted a young woman wearing a kimono and carrying a fan was likely a beloved souvenir of a trip to Japan.

These items had not become mere conversation pieces or reminders of happy times. They were necessary parts of the atmosphere of the home and they lived here in absolute harmony with the rest of the furnishings and *objets d'art*.

The musical ringtone of Becki's cellphone interrupted her characteristic design reverie. She had talked to Karl earlier. They were of course going to meet tomorrow morning at the wedding so it wouldn't be him calling again.

Do I even have time to talk to anybody else before we all head out?

Her heart beat a little faster.

"Hello."

"Becki, is she there?" It was Tony.

Tony knew the plan. Gina was on her way here and then they would drive to the church and meet him there. Just like on the big day. But Becki could tell from the urgency in his voice that he was alarmed for some reason. Normally wedding jitters were associated with the bride, weren't they?

"Gina's not picking up, Becki," Tony continued. "Has she got her cellphone turned off? Is she there with you?"

Becki felt her heart thud in her chest.

Damn it, I know this! Gina was berating herself for being so naive.

The first rule with regard to attempted abduction is never let yourself be taken to a secondary location. Scream bloody murder and fight as if your life depends on it. Because it might.

If no one notices you being snatched, who's to call the cops?

Even if your family and friends eventually report you missing, if you don't make a ruckus at the site of your kidnapping, there may be no clues left behind at the scene with which to look for you.

As a woman you've probably been raised not to make a huge commotion, so if a matter of life and death comes up, you're not immediately prepared to stand up vigorously for yourself. Your instinct is to wait and see and maybe you'll find a way to save yourself at the right time and place.

Fact is, more than likely you'll be taken to an even more isolated location where you will be even more vulnerable, and have even less opportunity for escape.

Tony lectured me on this time and time again. In fact, that's all he ever does is try to toughen me up.

But it all happened so quickly.

She was pinned down in the deep seat of the back of the car by the creep's massive legs. Her arms had been yanked behind her and they remained resolutely in his grip. She was painfully twisted toward the window, and all she could see of her abductor were pleated trousers, a brief span of finely knitted socks and large, polished leather shoes.

His awful men's fragrance filled her nose.

Her normal admiration for a fellow who looked after himself and was wearing expensive and well-kept clothes and stylish footwear morphed into revulsion. A disgust that manifested itself in the pit of her stomach and threatened to rise into nausea.

She guessed her initial shock was wearing off. She wanted to think it was replaced by a calm and rational evaluation of the reality of the situation but the truth of the matter was it felt more like panic.

My wedding tomorrow!

Gina, you have so much more to worry about than that!

I thought I knew Cathy!

What is she doing listening to this brute?

A victim like me?

She was fine in the store.

She was going to introduce me to her date.

She's dating the guy who tried to run over Sylvia?

Gina attempted to gather her thoughts, which spun a million miles an hour around and around in her head, to draw them into the centre.

He looks sort of familiar but, my God, I didn't get a very good look.

Wracking her brain, she wondered if she saw a picture of him on TV or in a magazine article or something.

Besides the wedding, what else have I been spending any time on?

Louisa's murder.

Does this have to do with the murder?

Earlier Becki had said, "In 97% of cases, the suspect is mentioned at some point during the first 30 days of the investigation."

Cathy knows this man.

Gina remembered a conversation in her condo.

Yes, a long time ago, Cathy was head over heels in love with Louisa's husband. They were having an affair.

Could this kidnapper be Garry Davenport?

He's supposed to be in jail for fraud.

The more I think about it, fraud doesn't carry a life sentence.

"I know who you are!" she shouted.

She was pleased that her voice didn't crack.

"Congratulations," he growled back. "That and a nickel will get you a cup of coffee."

Measured by the current cost of a cup of coffee, that's an ancient expression. That nailed it. *It fits. Garry wouldn't be a young man.*

Gina was restrained so low down—her head falling below the level of the car's windows—that she couldn't make "help me" faces at passengers in other cars on the road or at pedestrians walking along sidewalks.

From her point of view, the only objects she could make out were telephone poles, the tangle of wires that connected them and the crenellation of rooftops—some old, some new, some residential, some industrial.

Then she could tell by the surge of momentum that they were speeding along on a highway. Blue sky became visible. And a few billboards that must have been erected up high on embankments.

Finally there came an undeniable indication of their location—the thunder of a humongous jet airplane flying close to the ground.

It came into sight framed in the thick glass of the car window. Its bottom section hung low and its wheels were deployed like a giant Canada Goose coming in for landing.

While it passed right over top of them, Gina judged its flight path in relation to their direction of travel and calculated that they were on the 401, right along the airport in Mississauga, and heading west.

Definitely time to speak up again.

"Cathy, do you know that this car is wanted in connection to a hit and run that put a woman in the hospital?"

"No," Cathy said firmly, "I don't know anything about that."

From a sideways angle, Gina saw Cathy's head tilt up, then her eyes in the rear-view mirror, with a glance at Gina and then at Garry behind/beside her.

I can't make out the expression in her eyes.

"Is the blackmailing bitch dead?"

Gina decided she was going to go ahead and call him Garry. "No, Garry."

"Well then, she soon will be."

This did not bode at all well for Gina's own longevity.

"Listen to this guy, Cathy," Gina commanded. "See how violent he is? Call 911, then drive us to the nearest police station, or maybe a hospital."

"I'll break your neck right here and now if she tries," Garry threatened both Gina and Cathy.

"Garry..." Cathy seemed to be trying to soothe her ex-lover from the front seat. "We're planning to go to Rome, remember?"

Planning?

Present tense?

"Whatever trouble you're in, why don't you forget about it, and we'll soon be far away from everything."

With that, Gina decided to heap it on. She needed to get through to Cathy. "I think your boyfriend killed his wife. You better wake up, Cathy. Or you could be next."

"That's simply not possible," Cathy said, her words toneless. She kept on driving.

Garry muffled a snort.

Chapter 36

Black. That was the mood that coloured Tony presently. Pure black, and if anyone even tried to cross him now, they would feel his fist.

He was at the condo, pacing restlessly. They had decided he should stay there in case Gina phoned, while Becki drove to the church.

But Gina wasn't at the church. Becki had just phoned from there, and was still on the line. Everyone—all Gina's family, her parents, Uncle Jerry and Aunt Linda, Aunt Carla and niece Nellie—everyone involved in the rehearsal was gathered at the church.

Everyone but Gina.

"Where was the last place she was supposed to be?" Tony said into the phone. He fought to keep his voice cool.

"She was picking up my dress from the bridal shop, plus a few things of her own. Then we were going to all go together, from her parents. At least, I thought we were." There was a shaky tone to Becki's voice that betrayed her fear.

"Then we retrace her steps. Where's that bridal shop?"

"I'll come with you," Becki said. "The sales clerks will speak to me. You might frighten them."

Tony grunted. "On my way," he said, then clicked off.

The drive to the church was one he knew well. Years ago, he had been an altar boy there, with his cousin Ian. Many a confession had been blurted out to Father O'Flynn in those days when he was young and still going to mass. Later, older and definitely jaded, he had only graced the building for the odd wedding and one family funeral.

Funeral. His whole body tensed.

Becki was waiting outside at the curb. She pulled open the passenger door and threw herself into the seat.

As Tony shifted into first, Becki gave directions to Bella Sposa. She looked at her watch.

"It's a little after eight-thirty. They should still be there until nine."

Tony drove faster. He made a sharp right on College Street, veered north on Bathurst, then onto Bloor Street, weaving in and out of traffic like a Formula 1 driver. All the time, the pounding of his heart sounded way up to his ears.

At Becki's instruction, Tony turned off Bloor and onto a small side road. *Bella Sposa*, stated the sign to his right, illuminated from behind. He pulled around the back of the building.

"Look over there," said Becki, pointing. "What's that?"

Tony stopped the car beside something heaped on the driveway. A long grey garment bag.

Becki was out of the car and running. She reached the bag first, and didn't even bother to pick it up before undoing the zipper.

The maid of honour dress.

"That's it," Becki croaked. "My dress." She rose from a crouch, with the bag in her hands.

"She was here and she dropped it," Tony said. His stomach twisted. No way, would Gina drop a dress and just leave it there. *This was bad.*

"Her purse is here too, underneath. We need to ask inside. If they know anything," Becki said. She began to walk with Gina's purse and the garment bag in her arms. Then she scrunched it under one arm, and started to run.

The etched glass front door to Bella Sposa was cheerily bright. Becki bounded up the steps with Tony right behind her.

Once inside, Tony scanned the room. Only a few young women shoppers remained in the store. They twittered like little birds. Tony watched Becki as she sought out the elder sales clerk.

A big smile of recognition started on the older lady's face and then it changed to something like uncertainty.

"Can I help you?"

"You're Ilonka, right? You know Gina Monroe? I'm her matron of honour. Was she here earlier picking up my dress?" Becki was practically panting.

"Why yes! Is there a problem with it?" She eyed the garment bag in Becki's arms.

"She's missing," blurted Tony. "We need to know if she left here with anyone."

"She did," said Ilonka, clearly relieved. "She met a friend here. Miss Monroe waited for her to finish the fitting, and they left together."

Tony was about to burst with impatience. "What friend? What was her name?"

"Cathy," said Ilonka. "Cathy Spencer. I believe she is one of the wedding guests. Oh! And I guess you must be the bridegroom. How very nice to meet you." She held out a thin hand.

Tony missed it completely. His head whipped over to Becki.

"Yes. That would be our Cathy," Becki said softly, meeting his eyes.

She turned to the sales clerk. "Could you possibly give me her address? I have it at home, of course. It's just that I need to get in touch with Gina right away, and she's not answering her phone. It must have run out of power."

Becki was cunning, Tony had to admit. *Smart of her to handle this.* Even so, he saw a look of hesitation cross Ilonka's face.

"It's really important," Becki insisted. "It's about the rehearsal dinner."

"Oh!" said Ilonka. Her face relaxed. "Well, of course then. If she's a wedding guest, of course you have her home address. Silly me."

Ilonka walked behind the counter and slipped on the reading glasses that hung from a chain around her neck. Then she pulled open a drawer, fingered through slips of paper and pulled one out. With her right hand, she picked up a pen and started writing.

"Here you go," she said, handing Becki a white piece of notepaper with the store logo across the top.

"Thank you," Becki said. "I really appreciate it. You've saved me a trip."

"My pleasure," said Ilonka, removing her glasses. "Do send us a photo from the wedding. We love to display them in the store."

Tony was already down the concrete steps by the time Becki emerged from the store.

Twenty minutes later they were standing at the front door of Cathy Spencer's midtown house.

"No security system here," Tony noted with satisfaction.

"At least let me try the doorbell, before you break down the door," Becki said.

"The place is all dark. There's probably no one here, but just in case, we need to check every room for signs that Gina may have been here." Tony didn't want to say the worst. Not in front of Becki. "And I'm not going to break down the door."

Tony had taken a small brown leather case from the back seat of the car and was opening it now. "Keep a watch out, will you? Let me know if anyone comes within viewing distance, or seems curious."

"What are you going to do?" Becki hissed.

"Just keep an eye out."

Becki turned around to the watch the street, as ordered.

Tony wasted no time. It was an old fashioned lock, not one of those new electric ones, so he had the right tools. *Won't take a lot of time.*

And it didn't.

Tony was through the doorway in under two minutes. "You look around the main floor. I'll take upstairs." He raced up the carpeted stairs, leaving Becki flustered in the hall.

He started in the master bedroom, checking the closet, en-suite bathroom and each side of the bed. Then he meticulously made his way through the other two bedrooms and study.

Nothing.

He ran down the stairs, calling to Becki. "I'm going into the basement. You stay here."

At the bottom of the basement stairs, he momentarily held his breath. Usually he was cool in a 'situation,' but this was no ordinary emergency. This was where he might face his worst nightmare. He twisted the door handle and let himself in.

The basement was unfinished, which was not unusual in a house of this size. In front of him, row upon row of boxes lined up with precision, like little lines of soldiers. He checked down each path between them, and all around the walls of the basement.

Nothing. This time, he felt the relief spread across his face down to his throat.

He climbed the stairs.

No sound came from the main floor. "Becki?"

"I'm upstairs," she said. "Come back up."

Tony ran up the stairs, taking two at a time. Becki was in the master bedroom. She turned around when Tony appeared at the open door.

"Cathy packed to go away," she said. Her voice was firm.

"How do you know?"

Becki pointed to the walk-in closet. "There are a whole bunch of empty hangers in here. And a lot of her underwear is missing from the drawers."

Tony was baffled. "How can you tell that underwear is missing?"

Becki pulled open the right top drawer of the long dresser. "There's hardly any underwear in here. See? Every woman keeps the things she uses most in the top drawers. That's underwear." She pushed the drawer closed and moved to the closet.

"Maybe they're dirty?" Tony suggested.

Becki shook her head. "I checked the hamper over there. Hardly anything in it."

She walked back to the closet.

"See here?" She pointed to a shoe rack that spanned a three foot section of the large walk-in. "A bunch of shoes missing from the most reachable shelves. Cathy packed to go away."

Tony ran a hand roughly through his tangled dark brown hair. Where the hell did she go? And did she take Gina with her?

Chapter 37

The damned Echo scarf. When Gina had bought the thing—on sale—at Holt's, she'd never envisioned wearing it this way—stuffed in her mouth, with another scarf—Cathy's—tied around her face, holding it steady.

She was lying on her back on top of a motel room bed. Her hands were tied in front of her with duct tape. Ditto, her ankles. Not only were her wrists and ankles taped together, but he had rolled another longer length of tape horizontally so it formed a rope. And *that* was tied in a reef knot around the grey tape on her wrists and then around the closest bed post, where it bevelled in partway up.

Finally, Garry had wrapped her entire hands in duct tape, so she couldn't use her fingers to loosen the bonds. Not a chance she could work them free.

Luckily, her ears were still working.

After trussing her up, Garry had gone straight to the laptop on the little table and stayed busy there. Cathy was occupied with throwing clothes into suitcases.

Gina's mind was a wild thing, turning over alternatives. *They hadn't killed her.* That was the most important thing. If they were going to kill her, they would have done it right away. *So they didn't intend to.* Otherwise, they never would have taken her to the motel and tied her up like this.

No, they didn't intend to hurt her, of that she was now certain. Thank goodness she knew Cathy. Because there was no doubt in her mind now that Garry was a killer. And Cathy was, in her own convoluted way, protecting her.

Loyalty to a lover was one thing, but Cathy wouldn't let Gina come to any harm.

After a while, Cathy and Garry had retreated to the bathroom to talk. She strained with all her might to listen.

Cathy's voice was in hushed whispers, urgent, but the words were undecipherable through the wall. Gina strained, but couldn't hear Garry's baritone response.

She waited.

After a while, Cathy came out alone. She looked tired, and her eyes wouldn't meet Gina's.

"Don't worry," she said. "I won't let anything happen to you. We just need you out of the way for a while. So here's what's going to happen."

She took a breath and turned toward the sliding glass doors. She parted the drapes and seemed to be scanning the sky, which had darkened. "Garry and I are leaving the country. He's managed to change the tickets, so we have to run. We're leaving you here, but don't worry. The maid will come in about two hours to make up the room. They always do after you check out. She'll let you go."

Her eyes darted over to Gina, and then just as quickly, away.

The toilet flushed. And then Gina could hear the sound of water running.

Cathy turned back into the room.

"I know you'll probably call the police. I'm sad it had to be this way, Gina—really I am. I like you. And I know you don't understand. But I'm not going to lose Garry this time. I have to get him far away from here."

Her voice got a little softer.

"Garry explained about the car. I don't care what he's done. I love him. And if you really love Tony, you'll understand why I'm doing this. It's as simple as that."

Garry came out of the washroom. "Ready?"

Cathy nodded. She pointed to the suitcases, and then came back for her purse. She clicked off the light switch. Then she followed Garry out the door, without looking back.

The door clicked shut.

Once outside the room, Garry continued down the hallway, toward the front entrance. Cathy followed, then hesitated.

You couldn't die of thirst in a day. All they needed was one day. And she had just thought of a way to buy them a little more time.

"Just a minute," she said.

She walked to the door of the room just in front of her. It had a *Do Not Disturb* sign plugged into the card slot.

Cathy pulled it out, then went back to the door they had just exited. She slipped the sign into that card slot.

When she looked up, Garry was smiling at her.

"Good thinking, sweetheart."

It would be a lot more than two hours before someone came to clean out that room.

The first thing Gina felt was relief.

She was alone. No one could hurt her if she was alone.

The chamber maid would come. Cathy had said so. And Gina knew all about hotels. This was a motel, but surely they operated in a similar way. Now, she just had to wait patiently. Wait for the sound of the door opening.

The scarf in her mouth was soaked now. It tasted awful. But at least she could squish it forward to the front of her mouth, where it wasn't so choking. Thank goodness her nose wasn't plugged.

When her eyes adjusted to the dark, she tried to look around the room. Might be important to remember details of what the room was like, in case she was later questioned by the police.

It was a standard room with one king size bed. Colour scheme was sage green and burgundy...or maybe maroon. It was hard to tell in the dark. These colours were dominant in the dense, light-reducing draperies and the plush bedspread. The furniture was dark walnut in colour, and appeared fairly new. The television was wall mounted, maybe 32 inches. She couldn't see the rug. Not a particularly classy place, but it seemed clean.

A plastic clock-radio faced forward on the end table. She couldn't read the numbers because her head was drawn up too close to the headboard.

Now there was nothing to do but think.

She'd been avoiding that, because haunting her mind was something Cathy had said. "If you really love Tony, you'll understand why I'm doing this."

Did she really love Tony? If that was love, did she really love him? *Would she have kidnapped someone to protect Tony, if that's what it required?*

Now her thoughts were whirling.

Oh my God, Tony! Gina stiffened. He would be having a fit. Or wait—would he even know she was missing?

Becki. Becki would know. They were supposed to meet at her mom's at 7:30. Becki would sound the alarm when she didn't show up.

She was getting married tomorrow! Everyone would be at the church. She had to get out of here. There was so much left to do!

But most important, she wished to hell she had gone to the bathroom at Bella Sposa.

Minutes passed. Then hours. How many hours since she had been left here? And still no chamber maid. Still no sound of motel clients on either side of the room.

Occasionally, a car would drive by. Gina couldn't see it because, of course, Cathy had closed the drapes before leaving the room.

She felt weary and defeated. Stupid, stupid, stupid, for blurting out something so dangerous in the parking lot. Why hadn't she just noted the missing hubcap, smiled at the introduction, and hurried home to tell Becki and Karl? No question, she had a lot to learn about investigating people. Tony would laugh when he found out how incompetent she had been.

She was too keyed up and uncomfortable to sleep. Someone would come eventually. Might as well use the time she had usefully. *Think, Gina! Think back to the murder of Louisa Davidson.*

Garry must have done it. He must have found out where his ex-wife lived and driven up to Black Currant.

But wait. She wasn't his ex-wife! Gina kept forgetting that. *They had never actually divorced.*

So Garry had killed his wife. But why? Louisa was in hiding, so it wasn't as if she was expecting anything from him.

He'd already done his time. So it couldn't be a matter of suppressing evidence that would convict him.

Why would he kill her? Yes, she had the necklace and maybe more jewelry. But why would Garry kill her before she handed it over? Wouldn't he wait until after? And then, why bother at all?

But it had to be. For why else would Gina be lying here right now, after having recognized the car? Obviously, someone had tried to run down Sylvia because she saw something or knew something about Louisa's death. And that someone was also preventing Gina from going to the police right now.

It had to be Garry. It was Garry's car. But no matter what Gina came up with, she couldn't see a clear motive for Garry to kill his wife.

So, who? Who would have a motive?

And then she had it.

Chapter 38

They weren't going to Rome.

Cathy had figured that out when the car turned west on the QEW, instead of east. They weren't driving to Toronto International Airport.

"Where are we going?" she asked Garry.

A crooked smile crossed his face.

"Don't worry. I have friends you can't imagine," he said.

But worry she did. Gina would be free before long. The *Do Not Disturb* card in the lock would only keep the maid from cleaning the room. It wouldn't keep the room from being reassigned to a new arrival.

"Garry, we've got to get out of the country. Fast." Surely he understood that?

He just nodded. It seemed an under-reaction. But then, Garry didn't know the whole story. He didn't know about Louisa.

She hadn't told him everything. Even now she hesitated, not knowing how he would react.

Casting her mind back to that fateful day, she reminded herself that nothing *ever* goes as planned.

A week before Garry had been due to be released from prison, Cathy came alive. She was determined not to lose him again—not to jail, not to anyone.

So she set about to find out where his wife Linda had disappeared to.

It wasn't an easy task. But Cathy had the means to hire expert investigators, people who were professional skip-tracers.

They found her within days. And so Cathy drove to Black Currant Bay, to meet her rival in person.

Even now, she couldn't be entirely sure what she had hoped to accomplish by doing that. Maybe a simple reassurance that Linda would stand aside, and let her husband go free? Grant a divorce?

Nevertheless, Cathy was driven to face Linda and battle it out. She and Garry needed to be together—that's all that was important.

The confrontation in the Victorian kitchen had been brutal. Linda hadn't known about the affair. She had yelled and screamed at Cathy, called her awful names, horrible names, until Cathy couldn't stand it anymore.

She had tried to block out the hurtful words, especially the surprising information that Garry had sought out and spoken to his wife right there in that house before ringing her own bell.

Linda had even claimed, "Garry wanted us to try and work things out."

"I don't believe you," Cathy replied.

Linda rallied. "What? You think he really loves you, Cathy? Garry Davenport doesn't know the meaning of love. All he wants is money and power and—well—another word that starts with 'p'. An ugly, demeaning word I won't say out loud. But it's a word that suits you perfectly, my dear."

Was it unconsciously? Cathy wrapped the knuckles of her left hand around the top rung of the back of the kitchen chair next to her.

"Get out of my house!" Linda finally ordered. "Out with the trash! And tell your boyfriend not to come here again either or I'll disclose everything I have on him. Believe me, he doesn't want any more trouble to come his way."

Rage made Cathy invincible. Her right hand joined her left and she hefted the chair in the air.

A weak inner voice tried to stop her from proceeding any further but it could not compete with her fury.

Linda's fearful, pleading eyes were no contest either.

She bashed Linda over and over again as her rival cowered and backed away from her.

Eventually she had Linda cornered at the top of the cellar stairs.

One last thrust, one last ram, and she sent her toppling.

She hurled the chair after her for good measure.

A few moments later, with cold calm restored, she hugged the very edge of the staircase going down, hoping not to step in any blood if there was any. She checked to make sure Linda was gone for good. Then she grabbed up a few pieces of the broken chair, the parts that might have her prints on them, and she smuggled them away to be tossed at leisure.

Cathy hadn't told Garry about that. She wasn't sure she ever would.

But to be honest, he hadn't told her everything, either. What was all this about the car being in a hit and run accident? Who had been hit?

And why had Garry been so anxious to go to Gina's wedding? It was right out of character. What did he intend to pick up there?

Her mind continued to work over scenarios until Garry pulled off the highway. Before long they were traveling down country roads.

"Where are we going?" she asked Garry again.

"How do you feel about South America?"

Wow! That sounds exciting.

"I phoned ahead to arrange this flight and other connections. We don't go through normal customs this way," he said. "As I said, I have a lot of friends."

Friends in high places, she thought, as the car continued along unfamiliar rural roads.

"Don't worry too much about money, sweetheart. I've got enough to live where it's cheap, stashed away out of the country. Enough for us to live on for many years."

Cathy felt a jolt. She wouldn't be able to touch her own money, of course. They wouldn't want any traces left at this point. Such a shame.

But maybe later. Garry knew a lot of people. He could probably figure out a way to get at it.

"I'm just so damned sorry about the necklace, not to mention the other jewels," he muttered. "We should have the necklace. An extra four hundred thousand would make things easier."

"What necklace?" Cathy said.

Garry didn't answer. He turned the car down a laneway to a private airfield. Then he pulled up behind a small clapboard building that served as an office.

The next several minutes went by in a haze of activity. A young good-looking pilot was introduced. Money changed hands. Bags were swung from the car to a prop airplane close by. The pilot climbed on board to make preparations.

"It won't be long now, sweetheart." Garry put his arm around her waist.

"Going somewhere?" said a gravelly voice behind them.

She felt Garry stiffen. His arm left her as he whirled around.

"Johnny." His voice was a harsh whisper.

Cathy turned. The man who faced Garry was short, and heavy-set. His slick dark hair was a match for the expertly cut charcoal suit. Beside him stood a younger man, taller and definitely not as well dressed.

Beyond them, she could see a big black Mercedes, with the front and passenger doors still open.

The man called Johnny smiled with a lot of small white teeth. "Don't be so in a hurry. It's not healthy."

The air surrounding all of them had abruptly turned electric.

"You missed an important meeting," he continued. "My boss wants to talk to you. I got orders to make sure that happens." He patted the right hand pocket of his suit jacket.

Garry seemed to fold right before her. She watched in horror as his face crumbled into despair.

"How did you find me?" Garry asked finally.

The beefy guy shrugged and gestured to the air park office. "You're not the only one with friends."

Twenty-four hours was the time that police usually waited before acting on a missing person report. Tony knew this already. He didn't need Karl to tell him.

"That's ludicrous," said Becki. "We know she's missing *now!*"

Tony wasn't going to wait that long. All his training told him to move now. Get his contacts on it. Pull in every favour.

Fact. Gina was missing from her own wedding rehearsal.

Fact. Her purse and dress had been found on the parking of the bridal store, not far from her own car.

This wasn't a case of the bride getting the jitters and skipping town. You didn't leave your purse behind when you skipped town.

Gina wouldn't do that, anyway. *Not his Gina.*

Becki was staring at him strangely.

"Do you think there's any chance…" he started to ask her.

"No. Something has happened. Gina wouldn't leave without a word. For goodness sake, Tony, you *know* Gina."

Still, the doubts were there, tearing away at his already distraught mind. Yet, the alternative was worse. Gina getting cold feet was something he could handle. Gina, a cold body…

Action was the only way to keep the impending horror at bay. Luckily, Tony was a man of action.

He reached for his cellphone to get the ball rolling.

Chapter 39

It was probably not a civilized time of morning, but daybreak nonetheless. The blackout curtains couldn't completely hide the glow that was dawn. It seeped in around the edges and filled Gina with renewed hope and energy.

And urgency.

Oh yes, she was more desperate than ever to escape because this was the morning of her wedding, and also, to put it politely, she seriously had to relieve herself. Seriously.

She didn't know exactly how long she had gone without urinating. *But it must be going on three decades!*

Thank God she had not *added* to the nearly overflowing reservoir of her bladder since she left home last night.

One thing she knew for sure was that she'd better stop thinking about peeing.

Further subjects that are off limits—lakes, waterfalls, and...No crying either, Gina!

Suck. It. Up.

Had she tried everything that she possibly could to save herself last night after she finally realized it might take forever for the maid or anyone else to find her here? Damn it, yes! She would happily have gnawed through the tape with her teeth if she wasn't gagged!

There must be a way. There has to be a way.

Take for instance her fictional hero Jack Reacher—whose wandering habits and clandestine activities brought to mind the life she pictured Tony led when he 'previously' was working for Canada's federal agency—who always found a way. What would Reacher do? What would Tony do?

It only made sense that if, as it appeared, she'd used up her own bag of tricks, it was time to borrow someone else's.

Think like Reacher!

Wasn't he always lecturing about force in terms of mass and velocity or some such thing? Before launching into a dead run and using his six-foot-plus frame and his two-hundred-and-fifty-something bulk to kick through a door.

Didn't he also champion leverage in tricky situations?

Taking inventory, she realized she didn't have the advantage of much personal mass, and in her state, how could she achieve any significant velocity? But the more she thought about it, the more she thought she might be able to create leverage.

She didn't have a lot of leeway because the rope that secured her to the bed was only a foot long.

First she wriggled onto her right side. Now she had to bend in half. Bring her legs up so they'd be pushing against the bedpost while her arms pulled in the opposite direction.

Easier said than done.

When you're lying all trussed up, she discovered, moving your legs takes a whole lot of ab strength. More than she felt she could muster. On top of that, she literally didn't have all day to strain.

So she cheated.

She swung her bound legs like a canon across the night table, a movement that swept the cheap plastic clock-radio right off the smooth surface. It ended up stuck between the edge of the nightstand and the wall. *What good is a digital clock-radio that you can't read or listen to anyway?*

Still her feet—she'd long since lost her shoes in her struggles—were to the left of where they needed to be.

So she repeatedly and patiently flexed her abs and wriggled her body, moving closer to the position she desired.

She resisted the urge to kick indiscriminately.

Do not waste kinetic energy until you are properly set up, she told herself.

Finally, with knees bent and heels poised in front of the thicker upper length of the turned bed post, directly above where the rope was tied around a narrower groove in the column, she kicked with all her might at the same time as she yanked back with her arms, full weight behind the movement. Over and over in a synchronized fashion. She figured that eventually either the tape or—the furniture here couldn't be all that solid—the bed post would have to—

Crack!

The wood splintered and jagged shards shot out.

With continued pressure the post gave way completely, sending the upper part of her body flying back onto the cushion of the bed.

Yes!

But she still wasn't free.

Not free enough to leave the motel room and get to her wedding.

Not even free enough to use the toilet.

What next? Do I work on the duct tape myself or do I attract outside attention? Which is faster?

Last night, as much as she'd hammered on the wall behind her, no one had come to her rescue and it was obvious why. The bed was against the exterior wall facing the highway. No one there. But there were rooms on both sides of hers, and maybe some people in the hall.

Gina slithered off the edge of the bed until her feet touched the ground. She began to hop to the closest side wall but each bounce and landing cost her.

As she approached she also had to tell herself not to rush so she wouldn't lose her balance and fall on the ground. Who knew how long it might take to get up?

Once she faced her target, she thoroughly banged and thumped it.

Then she hopped to the door to the hall and did the same thing there.

Then she hopped through the bathroom on the other side of the room and continued banging. She would not give up until someone came to the door.

She still was thumping on the hall door when she heard voices directly outside. Immediately she took a hop back so as not to be knocked over when the door swung open.

But it didn't move.

"What's going on in there?" a man's voice shouted from the other side.

She couldn't answer.

"No one's answering," another man observed.

"Should we go in anyway?"

"Do you think it's dangerous?"

"Someone might be in trouble."

"Wish we could see through the curtains."

"Okay, watch yourself, I'm putting the key in the lock."

Finally the door flung open and Gina saw two guys backlit in a rectangle of light and staring in at her. They both appeared have taken up a fighting stance with their fists clenched, ready for action of any kind.

When they saw her, alone, they visibly deflated and rushed in to help.

One of the guys—he must have been the night manager because he wore a shirt with a logo on his pocket—pulled out a Swiss Army Knife. He slit the tape around her hands first.

While he was working on her feet, Gina ripped the scarf from around her head and pulled out the gag.

"Hurry please!" she said, her throat catching.

"Yes. Doing my best." The manager addressed the other fellow and said, "Thanks for coming and getting me, man."

Gina's feet broke free and she dashed to the bathroom, duct tape dragging behind her. She slammed the door shut.

When she came out, she knew the men would be full of questions but she didn't have time to stand and chat with them. She said, "Call the police. And call a taxi. Today is my wedding day." Then she demanded, "What time is it?"

Their eyebrows arched and their mouths fell slightly open. However, no matter how they were feeling, they did as she requested and called the police and a taxi service.

Afterward, the fellow who had alerted the motel manager offered, "Miss, right now it's about 9:00 in the morning."

"Oh my God! Oh my God!" Gina paced around the very small amount of space in the room. "My wedding is at 10:00 this morning at St. Francis of Assisi, College and Grace intersection, Toronto. Where am I?"

"Oakville."

"I'm a half an hour away! More if there's a lot of traffic!"

They nodded in agreement.

"I've got to call Tony. And Mom. And Becki. Where's my purse? Where's my purse?"

To her the two men remained unnervingly static while she raced all over the room looking in all the drawers, under the bed, even behind the shower curtain. "Where's my purse?"

When she rounded back on them they were standing with their hands up as if to say, "Don't look at me!"

"Will you lend me a phone?" she requested.

The night manager handed over his cell.

"Thanks," she mumbled. Then she froze. "All my important numbers are on speed dial on my own phone." She tried to punch in a couple numbers manually, by heart. She gave up when, through the still-open door, she saw a taxi driver about to knock.

"What time is it now?" she asked.

"9:17."

The police hadn't arrived yet.

"Tell the police I was kidnapped last night and brought here." She rounded up her pumps and shoved them on. "Tell them I'll be available to talk in a few hours but right now I've got to run."

She rushed past the door and out of her temporary 'jail', and as she did so she happened to notice the *Do Not Disturb* sign still plugged into the door's card slot.

Speaking of details, after the taxi had pulled away, she realized the two men she left behind to deal with the police wouldn't have much to work with. They wouldn't have the first clue who she was, even, because she hadn't given them her name. She'd been in such a rush that she also hadn't told them from where she was kidnapped. Or when.

Maybe the police would conclude it was a local *Fifty Shades of Grey* scenario gone wrong.

Chapter 40

No Vera Wang wedding dress, no Fiorio hair appointment, no Dior lipstick, no Chanel perfume, no nail file, no toothbrush, no pocket mirror to verify how the hell she looked.

How do you think you look after a night duct-taped to a motel bed?

No time.

It took superhuman willpower for Gina not to pester the driver to death about how much longer he thought it would take *now*.

Was she a fool to be hurtling toward the church? Would anyone even be there? How many brides who miss their own wedding rehearsal actually intend to show up at the wedding?

What was poor Tony going through? To think she'd had reservations about putting her faith in *him*.

On Grace Street in Little Italy, tears pooled in Becki's eyes and threatened to cascade down both cheeks at the tiniest provocation.

Gina.

Dressed in her recovered maid of honour dress—the Toronto police took some serious convincing to let her keep this evidence of Gina's disappearance—Becki paced back and forth in front of the arched doorways at the top of the steps to St. Francis of Assisi.

They could have cancelled the wedding of course. The bride was AWOL. But Becki would hear none of it. She believed that Gina would move heaven and Earth to make it to her wedding, if she possibly could.

Becki prayed as she patrolled the triple church entrances. Above her a cross-and-holy-book-carrying statue gazed out from a niche in the upper wall. St. Francis of Assisi himself she assumed. *St. Francis, help Gina make it here.*

Anything else was unthinkable.

Many of the wedding guests were already seated inside. Most knew nothing of what was going on. They were blissful in their ignorance. The few who did know didn't let on, just in case a rabbit could be pulled out of a hat.

As one of the co-conspirators in the charade, did Becki feel guilty about not advising all guests aforehand about Gina's potential no-show and thereby possibly saving their Saturday morning? Not one bit. Gina was all that mattered.

In the meantime, Tony had pulled in special favours. Karl too. Everyone was hunting madly for Gina. Judging by Tony's demeanor, it was the largest, fiercest missing-person investigation ever mounted.

Just as Becki and Tony had done themselves, Toronto police had interviewed Ilonka and the others at Bella Sposa where Gina was last seen about 7:00 p.m. yesterday. They had searched the store and its surroundings. They had canvassed neighbours.

Toronto police had gone further than what Becki and Tony and Karl were able to do on their own and broadcast Gina's description and all other pertinent information to officers in the field. They'd passed on that same information to surrounding police services.

Tony had shared his favourite cellphone picture of Gina with the Toronto police force, who were holding off printing missing person posters, interviewing family and requesting assistance from the media until after the wedding.

No one knew if Gina would show up. But they hoped. Now in this last fifteen minutes before the wedding there was a collective holding of breath. Becki identified in the others the same pent-up nervous energy that she felt in herself.

Every few minutes, she popped back into the church just to check. Bouquets of all-white natural flowers were tied with shimmery white tulle bows to the ends of the polished wooden pews all along the centre aisle. Becki and Gina had picked out the arrangements together.

In. Out. In. Out. Back and forth at the top of the stairs. Becki imagined Tony pacing in the back of the church just as she was doing in front. And what of Gina's parents? For now, Gord was sitting with Anna in their pew. How were they coping?

Outside again, Becki watched birds flit from towering tree branch to towering tree branch on this warm, sunny morning. By all appearances, a heavenly day.

Which only made things worse.

Tony and Karl had divulged their earlier plan to replace the real diamond and sapphire necklace set with a bugged fake, and have a couple guys stake out the church vestibule before, during and after the wedding. In these heightened circumstances, the undercovers remained in place, but they were the real jewels that nestled in the small box placed inconspicuously on the far end of the bench in the front entryway.

If that's what it took to save Gina.

Becki figured law enforcement was keeping an eye out for anyone or anything incongruous.

When she saw a familiar woman in turquoise, her skin prickled.

Lottie's mostly white hair was pinned in an up-do.

As nice as it had been for Lottie, among several of Becki's friends and acquaintances, to attend Gina's wedding shower in Black Currant Bay, Becki knew that the wedding guest list had not been revised to include Lottie at the ceremony here in Toronto. *Why was she here?*

Becki wanted to hurl herself down the stairs and grab the woman and shake the truth out of her. But she'd been drilled earlier this morning about what to do in a circumstance like this. Gina's life might be at stake.

She slipped into the shadows of the church foyer and let Lottie approach in the midst of other tardy guests.

Lottie was slower than the rest, who dashed up the stairs and into the main part of the church to find a seat. She paused, as if for air, during her ascent. Was she truly huffing and puffing or was she stalling for reasons of her own?

Becki continued to observe.

Lottie took one final look behind and around her before she passed the threshold of the church. Because it is generally expected that guests should be seated a good several minutes before the bride is due at the church, it would seem that Lottie was going to be the last of the arrivals.

When she turned right instead of heading down the aisle, Becki looked about frantically for the undercover cops. Where were they?

When Lottie sat down next to the package, Becki couldn't hold herself back. With lightning speed she got right into Lottie's face and with barely concealed venom, which she didn't realize she possessed, she ripped into her. "Tell me where Gina is!"

She wanted to physically rattle Lottie's bones, but she had been raised not to manhandle old ladies, or anyone else for that matter.

"Oh, Becki dear, isn't this a lovely church?"

Becki was not frightened of Lottie, who must not be aware that every element of her very proper attire was radically askew. Like Queen Elizabeth, only demented.

"Why did you choose to sit down here?" Becki demanded.

"Catching my breath, hon." Lottie looked up with woeful eyes. "Getting old is not for sissies."

Lottie was playing her part well. Convincingly. Non-threateningly. Now if Lottie clicked open her old-fashioned and therefore roomy handbag, and reached in, then maybe Becki should start to worry in a hurry.

Except she was sure the undercovers were watching and listening in the wings. And she could summon Tony anytime from the back of the church using the wireless connection he had rigged up to help catch the blackmailer, and much more importantly so she could alert him of any first glimpse of Gina.

She was about to commence accusing Lottie of killing her friend Louisa for the jewels to fund that crazy trip to Cornwall she blabbed about—of not finding the jewelry in the house after the murder, and somehow thinking that Gina had the pieces—of threatening Gina into bringing the jewels to her wedding—and of hiring someone to kidnap Gina—

Becki was getting a little confused.

Then Lottie hauled herself up. "Will you walk me down the aisle, Becki dear? Gina will be here any minute now and I certainly don't want to be back here making a nuisance of myself. You heard about those young men being arrested for the fire?" she continued.

Becki's thoughts were far away. "What?"

"Louisa's house. They found the nasty boys who did it."

This confrontation is not going at all the way I imagined, Becki thought.

"Hurry, hurry now dear." Lottie looked back through the open church doors and cried, "Gina's here!"

Chapter 41

Why didn't taxis have wings?

So much damned traffic on a Saturday. Who would have thought it?

Gina was free. She was elated. She was exhausted. She was beyond exhausted.

She was on her way to her own wedding.

Tony would be there. *Tony would damn well be there.* If he wasn't, she'd kill him.

No doubts now.

"Can you go any faster?" she begged the taxi.

Silly. Silly how you get caught up in the little things, squabbling and second-guessing each other.

Sometimes it takes a big thing to set everything all straight in your mind.

She and Tony were getting married today, and she wasn't waiting for anything, no change of clothes—no wedding ring, to delay it a minute.

As the cab driver swerved along city streets, Gina wondered where Cathy and Garry had gone. Would they ever be brought to justice? Probably not. Garry would have all the connections to make a clean disappearance.

Could she feel sympathy for Cathy? Maybe. Perhaps it had been an accident with Louisa. Perhaps they had quarrelled, and it got a little physical.

She certainly would feel that way about Tony, if some woman got in the way of them being together. *She knew that feeling.* It would be easy to get physical.

I must be going crazy here. There's absolutely no excuse for physical violence, except in a life-and-death case of self-defence.

The church was up ahead. Gina could see well-dressed people hurrying up the steps to the double doors. Lots of people. Too many people.

And then she saw Tony.

"Stop here," she yelled to the cab driver. "I'll be back in a minute with your fare."

The car stopped. The right rear door swung open and she bolted out of the back seat.

Then Gina ran. She ran, and Tony turned, and she ran right up and threw herself into his arms. He held her tight and she clung to him like she was never going to let go, not ever.

The first words out of her mouth were, "Have you got fifty bucks for the cab?"

Tony must have caught sight of Gina before overhearing Lottie say, "She's here!"

So there's no way he'd been in the back of the church as planned.

They had thought it would alarm guests to see a panicked groom pacing in front of the church so Becki was designated lookout. But it didn't surprise her that Tony was not where he said he would be. Of course he was skulking in the shadows at the side of the church with a view to the front.

Thank goodness Gina appeared to be okay!

Thank you, St. Francis. Although not a religious person, Becki clasped her hands and glanced upwards even as the most romantic scene she had ever witnessed played itself out on the steps of St. Francis of Assisi.

She gave Gina and Tony more than a few moments to themselves, while Lottie tottered off to find a seat.

Then she descended the stairs herself.

"Gina, I'm so glad you're here!" She opened her arms, and Gina let go of Tony and melted into her.

"God, I'm glad I'm here too."

Then Gina grabbed hold of Tony again, like she couldn't stop touching him, as if he might disappear in a puff of smoke.

Becki could only imagine what had happened to terrify Gina so.

And to delay her for fourteen hours. She had come close to missing her wedding, to losing the future she dreamed of.

But now she was safe, and things could be made perfect.

"I brought your dress," Becki offered. "And a bag filled with a whole bunch of stuff you might need. Say the word and I'll advise your guests that the ceremony will be delayed 15, 30 minutes. Whatever you need."

"What? I don't look like a bride?"

"Uh, you always look beautiful, Gina, but—"

"I thought *I* was the fashionista!"

Did Gina get hit on the head?

"Becki, I'm a changed woman. Nothing matters, nothing at all, except that I walk down the aisle right this minute and that Tony is waiting for me at the other end.

"Hand me my bouquet!"

Chapter 42

LIFE SECTION THE TORONTO HERALD

The Bride wore…Prada??

Deana Philpott, Society Maven

Last Saturday, in a daring switcheroo, fashion forward Gina Monroe ditched her Vera Wang original, and became Mrs. Tony Ferraro in a short Prada day dress.

Always the epitome of glam, everyone's favorite weather girl was expected to hit the church runway in full wedding frou-frou. Instead, our girl shocked the crowd with her simple look. Rumour has it that the bride went into hiding before the wedding to ensure she could pull off her plan.

Yesterday, I caught up with her by phone, dear readers, and here is what she had to say:

"For ages, I've worried about being too shallow, too obsessed with looks. Tony teases me about it. At one time, he said he would marry me if I were wearing a paper bag. So I decided to take him up on it. Not that a Prada dress is a paper bag, but I wanted to make a fashion statement.

"If you love someone, you don't need the finery and the fuss. It shouldn't matter what you look like on your wedding day."

Of course, our girl could never be anything but beautiful. But did you know she is also generous?

As for the Vera Wang, Gina Monroe—now Ferrero—is donating her pristine wedding dress to a charity auction soon to be announced.

We love our weather gal in Toronto.

Chapter 43

It was a sunny Sunday afternoon one month after their wedding, and they were lounging in her—*their*—condo, nearly falling off the too narrow couch.

"I never should have doubted you, Tony," Gina said.

"Shush," he replied. He smoothed strands of her hair back behind her left ear. Her head was tucked in close to his chest and his strong fingers caressed as if he were stroking a cat.

"Seriously, who else would dress up in a tux and wait at the church for his fiancée to show up after she stood him up at the wedding rehearsal?"

"Takes one hell of a fine man," Tony agreed.

So she punched him. A love tap, really.

They continued to reminisce about their wedding and everything that came before and after.

Gina recalled the original suspect list she and Becki had cobbled together.

ambulance crew
2 police officers
developer—Douglas Spellman
Lottie
entertainment mogul—Garry Davenport
mob
Cathy
Sylvia

They laughed at the 'ambulance crew' and '2 police officers' notations.

"How ridiculous!" Gina said.

"How Nancy Drew!" Tony said.

That merited another love tap.

"Spellman...now Spellman—"

"It's sometimes hard to tell a plain old jerk from a cold-blooded murderer, isn't it?" Tony said, his face a portrait of innocence when she turned toward him.

"You never know what lies beneath," Gina defended herself. "I bet you never pictured that dear senior, Lottie, as a jewel thief!"

"Got me there."

"Becki caught her wandering down Main Street, Black Currant Bay, after our wedding, wearing this amazing necklace and a pair of dazzling earrings. Totally incongruous with anything Lottie would wear on a normal basis, you understand."

"I find her story so sad," Tony admitted.

"You're right, dementia is terribly sad. They think poor Lottie wandered into Louisa's house in a sort of stupor, picked up the jewels and pocketed them.

"It may have made sense to her at the time. Or maybe it didn't. Hard to know. When pressed, she handed the jewelry back. It's anybody's guess who those gems will go to now. Maybe Lottie is mentioned in the will, which will finally be settled when the investigation is complete."

"I love how you wrote down 'mob' on your list. What do you think now?"

"I think Garry *was* involved with the mob. Probably with more than one crime outfit. Maybe that's why he's hiding out now."

"Not because he tried to run over Sylvia and because he kidnapped you?"

"That too. But not because he murdered his wife."

"Because he didn't. We know who murdered Louisa."

"We do," Gina agreed.

"Not Sylvia, the last name on your list."

"Not her."

"You told me what happened to her. She read about Gina's kidnapping and Garry's flight out of the country and finally came forward regarding who put her in the hospital."

"Yes," Gina stated the facts as she knew them, "before the murder, Sylvia witnessed Garry say to Louisa, 'If you change your mind, give me a call.' He opened his wallet, scribbled on a receipt and handed it over. Later while cleaning, Sylvia picked the note up from a side table, saw the phone number and added it to a neat pile on Louisa's desk."

"*After* the murder, when Sylvia thinks she's put two and two together, she goes back for the note."

Gina rolled her eyes. "She foolishly thought she'd make some money by blackmailing one of the biggest racketeers around."

"Garry couldn't risk being incriminated. Being sent back to jail. Do you think Sylvia has learned her lesson?"

"I think so."

"So that leaves Cathy. When did you decide it was her?" said Tony.

"After having been tied up for hours and hours, and stewing and stewing over how I got where I was. It was my love for you that set me on the right track."

"I like this part of the story. Tell me again."

"Some tough former federal agent you are!"

"I need to know it by heart so we can pass the tale down to our children."

"My blood was boiling," Gina explained. "I would willingly have eaten through duct tape to break away and get to you."

Tony squeezed her tight.

"I realized that hitting a woman over and over with a chair and shoving her down the stairs might have been the result of a similar feeling of desperation. A rage totally in the moment. The only highly emotional and interpersonal dynamic going on amongst our suspects was the one between Cathy and Garry. Who stood in their way? For the longest time, I was convinced Garry did away with his wife."

"Were you now?" Tony smiled.

"Then I played it from a different angle. My theory was cemented when I finally exited my prison and noticed the *Do Not Disturb* sign plugged into the door's card slot. Cathy had promised me the maid would come in about two hours to make up the room."

"She lied."

"And if you lie about one thing, it's highly likely you're lying about everything." Gina finished with a little self-satisfied nod.

"You want to know what I think?" Tony said.

Gina strained her neck around to look at him.

"We won't see those two again, but it won't be because they've left the country."

"Where...?"

Tony frowned. "You were right about the mob. I did a little asking around. Garry's connections go deep. He owed them a bundle, and now that he was out of the slammer, they wanted payback. That's where the jewelry came in. It doesn't pay to try to screw the mob."

"So you're saying justice will eventually be served."

Tony smiled. "Oh, a form of justice. Maybe not our kind."

Gina settled back into his arms. "And all over a silly necklace."

"Not silly," said Tony. "What did you girls call it? *Killer*."

~ * ~

If you enjoyed this book, please consider writing a short review and posting it on your favorite review site. Reviews are very helpful to other readers and are greatly appreciated by authors, especially me. When you post a review, drop me an email and let me know and I may feature part of it on my blog/site. Thank you.

mcampbell50@cogeco.ca or cynthiast-pierre@rogers.com

Message from the Authors

Dear Reader,

There are crimes of fashion, and there are crimes of passion. We have fun with the first, but are deadly serious about the latter.

The *Fashionation with Mystery Series* explores the kinds of passion that lead to crime. In A Killer Necklace, the second book in the series, murder is once more on the menu. Is it a small town murder? Or is this one imported, like haute fashion, from the big city?

We think you—like us—will conclude that passion knows no limits, wherever one lives. And we hope you will enjoy this second mystery in the series, as much as we enjoyed writing it.

Yours truly,

Melodie and Cynthia

Works by the Authors

Fashionation with Mystery Series
A PURSE TO DIE FOR (#1)
A KILLER NECKLACE (#2)

About the Authors

Melodie Campbell

Billed as Canada's "Queen of Comedy" by the Toronto Sun, Melodie Campbell achieved a personal best when Library Digest compared her to Janet Evanovich.

Winner of nine awards, including the 2014 Derringer (US) and the 2014 Arthur Ellis (Canada) Melodie has over 200 publications, including 100 comedy credits, 40 short stories, and nine novels.

Her first book, *Rowena Through the Wall*, was an Amazon Top 100 Bestseller putting her just ahead of Nora Roberts, and just behind Tom Clancy. Critics have called it "Outlander meets Sex and the City."

She is the Executive Director of Crime Writers of Canada.

melodiecampbell.com
fashionationwithmystery.com
Facebook: MelodieCampbellAuthor
Twitter: @MelodieCampbell

Cynthia St-Pierre

In marketing Cynthia wrote promotional, packaging and communications materials; penned articles for business periodicals; and a chapter of *How to Successfully Do Business in Canada*.

A member of Crime Writers of Canada, she has one award for fiction and has been a writing contest judge.

Best of all for a mystery writer, Cynthia has received a York Regional Police Citizens Awareness Program certificate, presented and signed by Julian Fantino, former Commissioner of the Ontario Provincial Police.

Cynthia grows vegetables in her backyard, makes recipes with tofu, and speaks English-accented French with husband Yves.

vegetariandetective.blogspot.com
fashionationwithmystery.com
twitter.com/stpierrecynthia (@stpierrecynthia)
google.com/+CynthiaStPierre

IMAJIN BOOKS ^{TM}

Quality fiction beyond your wildest dreams

For your next eBook or paperback purchase, please visit:

www.imajinbooks.com

www.imajinbooks.blogspot.com

www.twitter.com/imajinbooks

www.facebook.com/imajinbooks

IMAJIN QWICKIES ^{TM}
www.ImajinQwickies.com

CPSIA information can be obtained at www.ICGtesting.com
Printed in the USA
LVOW10s0909030416

481969LV00019B/711/P